The Devil's Arithmetic

HANNAH is to discover for herself the frightening reality of the tales her Grandpa tells of his times in the concentration camps. Suddenly, she is sucked from the safety of her family as they are gathered for their Passover Seder and finds herself living in Poland in 1942. Through strange and mysterious twists of time and fate. Hannah discovers that through her bravery and her caring, she too can contribute to the past and make the future a better place.

THE DEVIL'S

Jane Yolen

ARITHMETIC

BARN OWL BOOKS

*To my Yolen grandparents, who brought
their family over in the early 1900s, second class,
not steerage, and to my Berlin grandparents, who
came over close to that same time and settled
in Virginia. We were the lucky ones.*

*And for my daughter, Heidi Elisabet Stemple,
whose Hebrew name is Chaya.*

*And with special thanks to Barbara Goldin
and Deborah Brodie.*

First published 1988 in the USA by Viking
This edition first published 2001 by Barn Owl Books,
15 New Cavendish Street, London W1M 7RL
Barn Owl Books are distributed
by Frances Lincoln

Text copyright © 1988, 2001 Jane Yolen
Jane Yolen has asserted her right
under the Copyright, Designs and Patents Act, 1988
to be identified as the author of this work

ISBN 1 903015 10 3
A CIP catalogue record for this book
is available from the British Library

Designed and typeset
by Douglas Martin Associates
Printed and bound in Great Britain
by Cox & Wyman, Reading

Background

OF THE SIX MILLION Jews who died in the Holocaust, three million came from Poland, which had the largest Jewish population in Europe – Germany had less that half a million. The Jews of Eastern Europe spoke two languages, apart from the language of the country they lived in, Yiddish and Hebrew: Yiddish was the language of everyday life, Hebrew was the language of religious devotion. This is the story of one family living in a rural village in Poland during World War II.

Glossary

Passover – springtime festival to celebrate the liberation from slavery in Egypt

Seder – the ritual meal that begins Passover

The Four Questions – the questions the youngest person at the table asks the host

Bris – ritual circumcision

Malach ha-mavis – the Angel of Death

yarzeit – candle lit at the annual remembrance of the dead

Haggadah – the text of the Passover ceremony

yarmulke – skull cap

Affikonen – the piece of matzoh hidden during the Seder

kosher – food according the Jewish dietary laws

Chanukah – mid-winter festival of light

blood rituals – the accusation that Jews use Christian blood to make matzoh for Passover

Yiddish – the language spoken by Eastern European Jews

Chelm – mythical town in Poland populated by fools

Shadchan – marriage broker

shtetl – Jewish village

Rabbi – Jewish minister

pilpul – elaborate arguments, splitting hairs

schnorrers – scroungers

Yeshiva bocher – student of Jewish religion

schmatte – rag

rendar – the richest man in the village

goy – non Jew

mishagaas – a foolish act

Torah – Jewish holy texts

klezmer – Jewish music, often played at weddings

badchan – entertainer

shul – synagogue, place of worship

chaper – press ganger

bissel – a bit

shabbos goy – non Jew who lights fire etc. on the Sabbath

shikse – non-Jewish woman

Arbeit macht frei (German) – "Work Makes Free"

schnell (German) – quick

zugangi – newcomers

loym kristlichen – the wisdom of Christians

Achtung (German) – attention!

Sonder Kommando (German) – Jews who disposed of gassed bodies

musselman – one alive in body but spiritually dead

Ulith – Adam's first wife who turned into an evil spirit

blokova – female guard

drek – dirt

Kaddish – prayers for the dead

Gottenyu – God protect you

Ribono shel oylam – The wisdom of the universe

1

'I'M TIRED OF REMEMBERING,' Hannah said to her mother as she climbed into the car. She was flushed with April sun and her mouth felt sticky from jelly beans and Easter candy.

'You know it's Passover,' her mother said, sighing, in a voice deliberately low. She kept smiling so that no one at Rosemary's house would know they were arguing.

'I didn't know.'

'Of course you knew.'

'Then I forgot.' Hannah could hear her voice beginning to rise into a whine she couldn't control.

'How could you forget, Hannah. Especially this year, when Passover falls on the same day as Easter? We've talked and talked about it. First we've got to go home and change. Then we're going to Grandpa Will and Grandma Belle's for the first night's Seder.'

'I'm not hungry. I ate a big dinner at Rosemary's. And I don't want to go to the Seder. Aaron and I will be the only kids there and everyone will say how much we've grown even though they just saw us last month. And, besides, the punch lines of all the jokes

1

will be in Yiddish.' When her mother didn't answer at once, Hannah slumped down in the seat. Sometimes she wished her mother would yell at her the way Rosemary's mother did, but she knew her mother would only give her one of those slow, low, reasonable lectures that were so annoying.

'Passover isn't about eating, Hannah,' her mother began at last, sighing and pushing her fingers up through her silver-streaked hair.

'You could have fooled me,' Hannah muttered.

'It's about remembering.'

'*All* Jewish holidays are about remembering, Mama. I'm tired of remembering.'

'Tired or not, you're going with us, young lady. Grandpa Will and Grandma Belle are expecting the entire family, and that means you, too. You have to remember how much family means to them. Grandma lost both her parents to the Nazis before she and her brother managed to escape. And Grandpa . . .'

'I remember. I remember . . . ,' Hannah whispered.

'. . . Will lost everyone but your Aunt Eva. A family of eight all but wiped out.' She sighed again but Hannah suspected there was little sympathy in that sigh. It was more like punctuation. Instead of putting periods at the ends of sentences, her mother sighed.

Hannah rolled her eyes up and slipped farther down in the seat. Her stomach felt heavy, as if the argument lay there like unleavened bread.

It wasn't a particularly long trip from New Rochelle to the Bronx, where her grandparents lived, but the car

2

was overheated as usual and Aaron complained the entire way.

'I'm sick,' he said loudly. Whenever he was unhappy or scared, his voice got louder. If he was really sick, he could hardly be heard. 'I'm going to,throw up. We have to go back.'

As her mother turned around and glared at them from the front seat, Hannah patted Aaron's hand and whispered, 'Don't be such a baby, Ron-ron. The Four Questions aren't that hard.'

'I can't remember all four questions.' Aaron almost shouted the last word.

'You don't have to remember them.' Hannah's patience was wearing thin. 'You're supposed to *read* them. From the Haggadah.'

'What if I can't read it right?'

Hannah began to sigh, caught herself, and turned it into a cough. 'You've been reading right since you were three, Mr. Smarty.' She cuffed him lightly on the side of the head and he cried out.

'Hannah!' her father called back in warning.

'Look,' she said quickly to Aaron to shut him up, 'it doesn't matter if you make a mistake, Ron-ron, but if you do, I'll be right there next to you. I'll whisper it into your ear just like they do in plays when someone forgets a line.'

'Like Mrs. Grahame had to do when you forgot . . .'

'Just like that.'

'Promise?'

'Promise.'

She gave him a funny look and then pounced on

3

him, tickling him under the arms and over his belly. When he tried to escape by turning his back on her, she got him again from behind. His laughter rose higher and higher until he almost *did* throw up.

'Hannah!' her father said again and her mother stared at them so fiercely over the seat that they drew themselves into opposite corners, staring out their windows with expressions of injured innocence.

A few miles farther on, Aaron begged, 'Tell me a story, Hannah, please. Please. *Please.*'

'For God's sake, tell him a story,' her father said, pounding his right hand against the steering wheel. Driving in city traffic always made him cranky.

Glad to be doing something she knew she was good at, Hannah began a gruesome tale about the walking dead, borrowing most of the characters, plot, and sound effects from a movie she'd seen on television the night before. Aaron was fascinated by it. The zombies had just marched into the hero's house and eaten his mother when they arrived at the apartment house complex.

While their father parked the car, Hannah and Aaron raced into the building. Because he was the youngest, Aaron got to press the elevator button.

'That's not fair . . . ,' Hannah began. But then she remembered how scared she'd been the first time she'd had to ask the Four Questions at the Seder and she stopped. Instead she reached out and held his hand tightly as the elevator rose to the ninth floor in a single great swoop.

'Hannahleh, how much you've grown,' Aunt Rose said. 'Twelve years old and already a beautiful young lady.'

Hannah smiled and pulled away as soon as she could.

'Thirteen,' she said. It was almost true. She didn't ask Aunt Rose how anyone could be beautiful with mouse-brown hair and braces on her teeth. Aunt Rose thought everyone in the family was the *most* beautiful, the smartest, *the* greatest, even if it wasn't true.

Escaping Aunt Rose's attentions by going into the bathroom, Hannah looked at herself in the mirror. There was a lipstick stain where Aunt Eva had kissed her on the forehead. She ran some water and tried to scrub it off, feeling guilty because Aunt Eva was her favorite aunt, the only one who preferred her over Aaron. Hannah was even named after some friend of Aunt Eva's. Some *dead* friend. The lipstick wouldn't come off completely. Brushing her bangs to hide the mark, Hannah left the bathroom worried that someone else might be lying in wait for her, and dreading it.

2

NO ONE EVEN NOTICED Hannah's entrance into the living room. They were all in a tight semi-circle around Grandpa Will. He was sitting in the big over-stuffed chair in front of the TV set, waving his fist and screaming at the screen. Across the screen marched old photos of Nazi concentration camp victims, corpses stacked like cordwood, and dead-eyed survivors. As the horrible pictures flashed by, a dark voice announced the roll of camps: 'Auschwitz, Bergen-Belsen, Chelmno, Dachau . . .'

'Give them this!' Grandpa Will shouted at the TV, holding up his left arm to the set. The sleeve of his shirt was rolled up above the elbow. The photograph of a Nazi colonel, standing sharply at attention, flashed by. 'I'll give them this!'

Aunt Eva was shaking her head as Uncle Sam, snapped off the TV set. Then she murmured, 'Please forgive him, please. It was the war.' Her voice was as soft as a prayer.

Hannah sighed. 'He's starting again,' she whispered to Aaron.

Aaron shrugged.

Hannah could scarcely remember when Grandpa Will didn't have these strange fits, showing off the tattoo on his left arm and screaming in both English and Yiddish. When she'd been younger, the five-digit number on his arm had fascinated her. It was a dark blue, very much like a stain. The skin around it had gotten old, but the number had not. Right after Aaron's birth, at his *bris* party, when all the relatives had been making fools of themselves over him, Hannah had taken a ballpoint pen and written a string of numbers on the inside of her own left arm, hard enough to almost break the skin. She had thought that it might please Grandpa Will as much as the new baby had. For a moment, he'd stared at her uncomprehendingly. Then suddenly he'd grabbed at her, screaming in Yiddish *Malach ha-mavis* over and over, his face gray and horrible. Everyone at the party had watched them. It had taken her father and Aunt Eva a long, long time to calm him down.

Even though they tried to explain to her what had upset Grandpa Will so, Hannah had never quite forgiven him. It took two days of hard scrubbing before the pen marks were gone. She still occasionally dreamed of his distorted face and the guttural screams. Strangely, though she'd never dared ask what the words meant, in her dreams she seemed to know. No one had ever volunteered to tell her. It was as if they'd all forgotten the incident, but Hannah had not.

'Mama,' Hannah said when the TV was turned off and calm restored at last to the room, 'why does he bother with it? It's all in the past. There aren't any concentration camps now. Why bring it up? It's embarrassing. I don't want any of my friends to meet him. What if he shouts at them or does something else crazy? Grandpa Dan doesn't shout at the TV or talk about the war like that.'

'Grandpa Dan wasn't in the camps, thank God. He was born in America, just like you. That's because my family came over to this country in the early 1900s, second class. Not steerage.' She got that faraway look that signaled she was about to recite another part of the family saga.

Hannah knew there was only one escape.

'I think I'll help Aunt Eva in the kitchen,' she said quickly, and ran from the room before her mother could continue.

Although it was Grandma Belle's place to light the candles in her own home, over the years it had become a family tradition to let Aunt Eva do it, compensation for her not having a house or family of her own. Aunt Eva could have been married, not once but three different times even though, as Hannah's mother had pointed out, she was no great beauty. But Aunt Eva had preferred living with her brother, Will, and his wife and helping them raise Hannah's father when Belle was away at work.

'Why did she do it?' Hannah had often asked.

'Because she wanted to' was the only answer her father had ever given.

'Maybe she likes kids,' Rosemary suggested once. 'Maybe she likes cleaning house. I have an aunt like

8

that.'

'And what does she do?' Hannah had asked.

'She's a nun.'

'Don't be a jerk. Jews don't become nuns.'

'So they live with their brother and take care of his kids.'

'His kid,' Hannah said. 'My father's an only child.'

But none of the answers satisfied Hannah's need for romance and a perfect story. Still, she eventually stopped asking the questions, and the only issues she ever brought up with Aunt Eva herself had to do with everyday things. Like how many teaspoons of sugar went into a glass of iced tea. Or what took a stain out of a leather skirt. Or how to knit a scarf. Or make potato soup. Or where to find a pair of old-fashioned shoes for the school play. Aunt Eva had always had the answers to those sorts of things.

When Hannah had been younger, Aunt Eva's answers had seemed magical. But as Hannah got older, the magic disappeared, leaving Aunt Eva a very ordinary person. Hannah hated that it was so, so she pushed the thought away.

Still, when Aunt Eva lit the holiday candles, broad hands encircling the light, her plain face with its deepset coffee-colored eyes took on a kind of beauty. The flickering flame made her look almost young. Watching Aunt Eva saying the prayers over the candles was the one moment in all the family gatherings that Hannah had always found special. It was as if she and her aunt shared a particular bond at those times, as if the magic was still, somehow, alive.

'A *yahrzeit* for all the beloved dead, a grace for all the beloved living,' Aunt Eva always whispered to Hannah before reciting the Hebrew prayers. Hannah whispered along with her.

Even Aaron tried to get in on the act, but he mumbled the words a full beat behind. Annoyed, Hannah poked him in the side, but he shifted away. In frustration, she caught up the fleshy part of his upper arm between her fingers and pinched. He cried out.

'Hannah!' her father said sharply.

Hannah felt her face grow red and she looked down at her plate.

3

DURING THE ENDLESS Seder dinner and the even more endless explanations from the Haggadah, Hannah frequently glanced out the window. A full moon was squeezed between two of the project's apartment buildings.

Her grandfather droned on and on about the plagues and the exodus from Egypt. Maybe it was an interesting story if someone else told it, Hannah thought, but Grandpa Will had a voice that buzzed like the plague of locusts, and he made sour lessons at every pause. The Seder wasn't even in the right order, not like they taught in Sunday school. When Hannah tried to protest, she was shushed down by Uncle Sam.

'It's Will's way. Don't make trouble,' he said.

Hannah stared at the moon. Tomorrow they'd be going to Grandpa Dan's for the next Seder. At least there would be three cousins her own age, all boys, but that couldn't be helped. And they'd get to sit at the kitchen table away from the grown-ups. And Grandpa Will wouldn't be there shouting and making a scene, only Grandpa Dan. Sweet, gentle, silly Grandpa Dan, who told stories in between the read-

11

ings and said things like 'How do I know? I was there!'

Beside her, Aaron was moving restlessly, getting ready to ask the Second Question. With the *yarmulke* covering his fair hair, he looked like a miniature Grandpa Will. Hannah almost laughed aloud remembering what Rosemary had asked at her first – and only – holiday visit: 'Why do they wear those beanies?'

Aaron's hands shook and a page in the Haggadah flipped over by itself. Hannah reached out and smoothed it back for him and he smiled up at her gratefully. He has the greatest smile, Hannah thought. *He* won't need braces.

'Stop worrying,' she mouthed at him.

At her urging, he plunged into the Second Question, chanting the Hebrew perfectly because he'd memorized it. But when he looked down at the book to read the English translation, he stumbled over the word *herb*, pronouncing the *h*. Uncle Sam snorted and Aaron stopped, mortified. He looked around the table. Everyone was smiling at him. It was clear that he'd made some silly mistake, but he didn't know what it was he'd done. He turned helplessly to Hannah.

''*Erb*,' she corrected with a whisper. 'Don't pronounce the *h*.'

He nodded gratefully and started on the English again, finishing too loudly and in a rush, a sure sign he was unhappy. 'On all other nights we eat vegetables and '*erbs* of all kinds. Why on this night do we eat bitter '*erbs* especially?'

Why indeed, Hannah wondered. *Since they're so disgusting. Rosemary gets to eat jelly beans and I get to eat horseradish.* 'It isn't fair!' She realized suddenly that she'd spoken the last words out loud and every-one had heard. Embarrassed, she stared down at her hands, but her anger at the injustice continued.

'Of course it isn't fair,' whispered Aunt Eva to her, 'but what has fair to do with it?' She smiled and, to break the tension, started singing 'Dayenu' in her strong, musical voice. The rousing repetitive song carried them all along, even Hannah's mother, who was tone deaf.

> *Da-da-yaynu*
> *Da-da-yaynu*
> *Da-yaynu, Da-yaynu.*

Hannah knew it meant 'it would have been enough,' but she suddenly felt that nothing was enough except to get out of that room and that Seder in which nothing fair or fun was happening.

And then she remembered the wine. That, at least, was new. When the Seder began again, she would get another glass of watered wine. For the first time, she was being allowed to drink along with the grown-ups.

'Let Hannahleh join in the toasts for real,' Grandpa Will had said before the Seder had begun.

'Now, Poppy,' Hannah's mother protested, 'she's only twelve.'

'Thirteen,' Hannah said.

Eva had patted her hand.

'And when my sister Eva was thirteen, what she would have given for a little glass of watered wine . . .' Grandpa Will had begun. It was the same

13

kind of argument he used for everything. He never had to finish the sentence, for no one could withstand the promise of guilt.

'All right, Poppy.'

Grandpa Will had smiled, turning to Eva. 'See, they can't keep her a baby forever.'

Babies, like Aaron, had to make do with grape juice. Hannah had been grateful to her grandfather for that. And she had discovered, with the very first toast, that she liked the sweet, cloying taste of the wine, even. though it made her head buzz.

'Hannah!' Aaron tugged on her sleeve and his eyes were, full of mischief. 'It's time.'

'Time?' For a moment she thought he meant time for the next toast, and then she realized he meant time to steal the *afikoman*, the matzoh wrapped in the blue embroidered cloth. Looking around the table, she saw that the adults were all suddenly very busy talking to one another. She remembered when, as the only child, she'd been the one to take the *afikoman*; she'd thought herself terribly clever when she found it under Grandpa Will's chair. Of course, now she knew that he always hid it there for easy discovery. She smiled at Aaron, suddenly feeling very adult. 'You go look for it. I'll keep watch here.'

'Okay.' He slipped from his chair and crawled around to the head of the table. Then he leaped to his feet, holding the blue cloth and its crumbling contents high over his head. 'I found it, Poppy! Now I get to hide it.' He ran from the room, but no one leaped up to follow.

14

'He's going to hide it in the bathroom,' Hannah said to no one in particular. 'He always does.'

'Hush, Hannahleh, don't spoil things,' Aunt Rose said.

'You always hid the *afikoman* under Grandma Belle's pillow,' Aunt Eva said.

'You knew?'

Uncle Sam guffawed. 'You left enough crumbs.'

'Knowing and not-knowing,' her mother said and sighed. 'It's all part of the game. And the game is to uncover the hidden order of the universe. Seder means "order." I read that in a book.'

'What hidden order?' Grandpa Will said. 'Do you think there was order back in the camps? Do you think . . .'

Eva interrupted smoothly. 'Lily, Lily, you are much too serious about these things. Let the children play. They are children for such a short time. And it's not as if we keep kosher or do things as a rabbi would. We do it *for* the children. Isn't that right, Belle?'

Grandma Belle nodded. 'So they can have fun *and* remember their history.'

Brushing the stray wisps of white hair from her broad forehead, Eva rose. 'Here we come, Aaron, ready or not.' Signaling the others to follow her, she left the dining room.

The men stayed at the table talking, but Aunt Eva and Aunt Rose went into the bedroom in a noisy search. Hannah's mother was almost as loud looking about the kitchen. They spent minutes calling out to each other about how difficult Aaron was to find this year, until Grandpa Will put his fingers to his mouth and let out a piercing whistle that brought them all back.

Hannah had been waiting at the bathroom door as if on guard. At the whistle, the door opened and Aaron peeked out.

'Hannah, I'm in here,' he whispered.

'Big surprise,' Hannah said, slipping into the room.

'Look where I hid the *afikoman*.' He took the blue cloth out of the dirty clothes basket.

'That's disgusting, Aaron, hiding it in someone's laundry.'

'They never even looked in here, Hannah. I flushed the toilet and pretended to be going, and no one came in.' He grinned.

'You're so smart, Ron-ron.' Hannah had to laugh at his earnestness. 'What are you going to ask Poppy for?'

'A baseball glove.'

She knew how much he wanted one. He'd been saving his Chanukah money and doing extra chores.

'Good choice,' she said. 'No matter what Poppy offers you to buy back the *afikoman*, you hold out for that glove.' She looked at herself in the bathroom mirror, wondering when the braces would come off. This summer, if she was lucky. 'I got a Barbie doll dress collection once.' She didn't admit that she'd regretted it right after. When she turned to say something else, Aaron was already gone.

The rest of the Passover meal was tempting, but Hannah had eaten so much at Rosemary's, she only picked at her food. Besides, her head was beginning to throb.

Uncle Sam poured another quarter glass of wine into her glass, then filled it the rest of the way with water for the next blessing. Suddenly she was sure she didn't want any more.

'My head feels funny,' she said to her mother.

'I told you she was too young for wine,' her mother said with a sigh. 'Even watered wine.'

Uncle Sam handed around the large cut-crystal goblet, Elijah's cup, and everyone poured a little bit of wine from their own glasses into it. When it was Hannah's turn, she emptied her entire glass.

'Elijah can have it all,' she said grandly.

Grandpa Will smiled down the long table at her. 'What a good girl. For being so unselfish, *you* can open the door for the prophet and welcome him in.'

'I wanted to do that,' Aaron called out. 'That's the most fun.'

'Hannah will do it, Aaron,' Grandpa Will said, 'because she was so generous with her gift.'

'He can have my whole cup, too,' Aaron said.

'A sacrifice unasked is so much the greater,' Grandpa Will stated flatly. 'Come, Hannah.'

Hannah stood reluctantly. She felt like a fraud. She hadn't given the wine out of generosity, but only because she didn't want it. It was no sacrifice.

'Remember, Hannahleh, we open our door to remind ourselves of the time Jews were forced to keep their doors open to show the Christians we were not practicing blood rituals. Hah!' His last syllable was a noisy punctuation. 'As if we were the bloody ones . . .'

Aunt Eva leaned over and laid her hand quietly on his. It was enough to calm him. He smiled 'Open the door to Elijah, child, and invite him in with an open heart.'

Slowly Hannah moved toward the front door, feeling incredibly dumb. She certainly didn't believe that the prophet Elijah would come through the apartment door any more than she believed Darth Vader, or Robin Hood, or . . . or the Easter Bunny, would. No one believed those superstitions anymore. No one except babies. Like Aaron.

Glancing over her shoulder, Hannah saw they were all watching her intently. Aaron bounced up and down on his chair.

'Open it, Hannah!' he called out loudly. 'Open it for Elijah!'

Baby stories! she thought angrily, unlatching the double bolt. Flinging the door open wide, she whispered, 'Ready or not, here I c . . .'

Outside, where there should have been a long, windowless hall with dark green numbered doors leading into other apartments, there was a greening field and a lowering sky. The moon hung ripely between two heavy gray clouds. A bird pelted the air with a strange, lilting song. And across the field, stepping in the furrows, marched a shadowy figure. He had a shapeless cap on his head, a hoe over his shoulder, and he was singing:

Who asked you to be buried alive?
You know that no one forced you.
You took this madness on yourself.

4

'HOW DID YOU DO THAT, GRANDPA? Hannah
asked, turning around.

Behind her the elegant meal, with its many plates,
goblets, glasses, and silverware, was gone. Instead
there was a polished table on which a single wooden
bowl sat between two ornate silver candlesticks. A
black stove, pouring out heat, squatted against the far
wall. There were shelves on either side of the stove,
filled with crockery, pots, and linens. Several strings
of onions hung from the ceiling. The room smelled of
fresh-baked bread.

It must be the wine, Hannah thought. *It's giving
me daydreams.*

'Well?' The question came from behind her in a
woman's voice, strongly accented. 'Is he coming?'

Confused, Hannah looked around for the speaker.
'The prophet Elijah?' she asked.

'And do you think the prophet Elijah walks in every
time you open a door? *A goy zugt a vertl*, there's a fool
in every house.' The woman was dressed in a dark
skirt covered with a smudged apron, an embroidered

blouse with the sleeves rolled up, and a blue kerchief on her head. Her bare arms were dusted with flour. Standing at a low table near a sink, she was pounding bread dough.

Hannah was stunned. It was as if she'd suddenly been transported to a movie set. The illusion was so complete, she couldn't even find an answer. And then the words the woman had spoken came to her: *a goy zugt a vertl* . . . It was a Yiddish phrase her grandfather used all the time and which she'd never understood before. Yet now it was as clear as if she could speak the language herself. *A goy zugt a vertl* meant 'As the peasant says . . .'

'So, Chaya, is Shmuel coming or not?' The woman did not look up from the dough as she spoke but continued to beat it with a steady, hypnotic rhythm.

Hannah looked out the door again, as if it could offer her some clue. Since she'd opened one door and entered this daydream, perhaps going through another would bring her home again. It was worth a try. Taking a step forward, she saw that the man crossing the field was much closer now. She could make him out clearly. He had a thick black beard and a full head of black hair topped with a cap. His shirt was full-sleeved and the loose-fitting trousers were pushed into the tops of high leather boots. *What Rosemary would give for such boots*, she thought. The man was no longer singing but was whistling a vaguely familiar song. When she realized it was 'Dayenu,' she laughed.

'Oh, I get it,' she muttered, though she didn't really. But she decided in that instant to play along.

21

Whether it was a dream or an elaborate game, she'd show them all she was a good sport. It was certainly better than Grandpa Will's deadly dull Seder lessons. 'He's coming,' she said, turning back to the woman.

'Good. Set the table. And be sure to use the Sabbath cloth. This is a special occasion, after all. It's not every day my baby brother is to be married the next morning.' She wiped her hands on the apron. 'Well, Chaya, move!'

Chaya. But that's my Hebrew name, Hannah thought. *The one I was given to honor Aunt Eva's dead friend. Weird.* She wondered how the woman knew that name, then laughed under her breath at her own foolishness. *Of course the woman knew. She was part of this crazy game. This crazy dream.* But even as she thought that, Hannah felt a panic pressure in her chest. Where *was* she? And where were her parents and Aaron and Aunt Eva and the others? She stared at the door again as if it held the answer.

'Why are you standing there looking like a Chelm fool, Chaya? The cloth, child. I swear, the fever that carried your poor parents off – may they rest in peace – has done you more damage than we thought. It was a miracle you survived at all. And while that was surely part of God's orderly plan, its meaning is beyond me. Sometimes, child, you make me wonder.'

Whatever it was the woman wondered never got said, for just then the bearded man marched into the house, having dropped his hoe somewhere outside. He grabbed Hannah before she could protest and spun her around.

'Hallo, little niece. Give your almost-married Uncle Shmuel a hug!'

Hannah knew she had no Uncle Shmuel, certainly no one as big and bearded as this man, who smelled of sweat and grass and horses. But his joy was contagious. She gave him a hug.

'Put her down, Shmuel!' the woman scolded. 'She's still recovering from her illness. You know how easily she gets upset and forgets things. And go wash yourself. I wonder that Fayge ever accepted the *shadchan*'s offer for your hand in marriage. You are so much of a prize you can kiss women without bathing?' She held out a large flowered bowl filled with water.

'Not such a prize?' asked Shmuel, as he dipped his hands into the bowl, slopping water over the side. 'I have all my teeth and all my hair, two fine workhorses, a four-room house, and twenty acres of land beside. I work hard and I do not smell all that bad, eh, little Chaya?' Without waiting for her answer, he lifted the water to his face and continued washing noisily.

'What is the child going to say, Shmuel? She adores you. But it will be very crowded in this house with another woman if you do not bathe regularly. Even though the new woman is that jewel Fayge.'

Shmuel reached out and pinched his sister on the cheek. 'Do you adore me, too, Gitl!' he asked, laughing fondly.

Annoyed, she drew back from his touch and a pin shook loose from her hair. Making a wry mouth, she removed her kerchief and drew out the other two pins. Her thick black hair cascaded down to the small of her back. 'I adore any of my brothers the day before they get married,' she said. Then with a swift movement, she wrapped the hair around her hand into a bun, which she pinned on top of her head again. She put the kerchief back over the hair and knotted it securely.

Hannah watched silently, trying to take it all in. How could she be both Hannah and this Chaya whose parents had died of a mysterious disease? She *knew* she was Hannah. She knew because she remembered. She remembered her mother and her father and her brother Aaron with his big blue eyes and great smile. She remembered her house with the junglegym in the backyard and the seventeen stuffed dogs on her bed. She remembered her best friend Rosemary, who'd had braces the year before she did and had showed her how to eat jelly beans with them on, even though you weren't supposed to. She remembered her school in New Rochelle. As she remembered, she forgot to be a good sport and her eyes began to fill with tears.

But the man Shmuel and the woman Gitl didn't seem to notice. They were too involved in their own conversation.

'If you would accept Yitzchak the butcher's offer, you could be married, and living in a fine new house in the center of the shtetl,' Shmuel said. 'Then you would not have to share your kitchen with Fayge or anyone else.' He turned and winked at Hannah.

'Yitzchak the butcher is a monster. All he wants is a nurse for his children.'

'All butchers are monsters to someone who refuses meat,' Shmuel said. 'And he only has the two children, not an army. They are young enough so you could be a real mother to them and you are young enough so you could give him even more.'

'Hah!'

Shmuel turned and smiled at Hannah, signaling her closer to his side. She was hesitant to go. What if by moving closer to him she became more Chaya and less Hannah? What if by accepting the reality of the dream, she lost her memories of her actual past? She wouldn't move. No one could make her. But Shmuel's smile was so genuine. It reminded her of Aaron's. He held out a hand.

'Come, Chaya, or do you think me a monster like Yitzchak?'

She moved.

Close up she could see there was a band of paler skin around his forehead, which his cap must have kept shaded from the sun. And he had the bluest eyes she'd ever seen, bluer even than Aaron's.

In a loud conspiratorial whisper, Shmuel said, 'She is still waiting to hear from Avrom Morowitz, who went three years ago to America, promising to send for her. But why should he send for her when he has not bothered to send even so much as a letter . . .'

'I would not go to America for Avrom Morowitz even if he sent a thousand letters. I will live and die in this shtetl, as did our parents and as did their parents before them. That is how it should be.' Gitl's mouth was set in a firm line, and she shook her finger at her brother.

Shmuel began to laugh, letting it start deep down in

25

his belly and then rise higher and higher. After a bit, Gitl joined in. At the last, the two of them were laughing so loudly they were almost paralyzed by their own silliness.

Poker-faced, Hannah stared at them. Nothing they had said seemed at all funny, but that she'd understood them at all seemed miraculous. For the more they talked, the more she realized they were *not* talking in English. They were speaking Yiddish. And yet she could understand it, every word. Perhaps of all the strange things in the dream, this was the strangest.

She suddenly remembered going to the United Nations with her fifth-grade class and sitting in the big council room. The different representatives had all spoken their own languages – French, Spanish, Russian, Chinese. And she'd listened with earphones that carried translations of each speech. With one earphone off, she could hear both languages going at once. It had fascinated her. This was a lot like that, except that the English translations were going on simultaneously in her head. It was totally illogical. But dreams, it seemed, had their own logic.

She must have made a noise, some small whimpering, because suddenly both Gitl and Shmuel stopped laughing and looked at her with concern.

'What is it, child?' Gitl asked. 'Are you all right? Does anything hurt?' And when Hannah managed to shake her head, Gitl turned to her brother. 'I swear, Shmuel, city living does damage to the soul. When our brother Moishe and his wife – may they rest in peace – left for Lublin, they had happy souls. And their little

Chaya, so they wrote, laughed all the time. But this grave little whimpering bird is out of a sorrowing nest. Look at her. Look.'

Shmuel put a protective arm around Hannah. 'She has been through a lot, Gitl. And remember how you and I and Moishe were when our parents died, and we so much older at the time, too. Besides, she is still not recovered in her strength. Do not worry. She'll smell the good country spring and eat new-laid eggs. She'll help you with the housework and me with the plow. We'll put weight on her and color in her cheeks. The laughter will return.'

'From your lips to God's ears,' Gitl said. 'For He certainly knows there's enough sorrow in the world. In the countryside as well as the city. Especially these days when laughter is our only weapon.'

Shmuel laughed. 'Do not let Fayge's father hear you say that. He insists only studying the Torah will do.'

'I hear Reb Boruch is a solemn man,' Gitl said carefully.

'Solemn! He would make a donkey look like a joker,' said Shmuel.

'Shmuel, that is your father-in-law you are talking about. The good rabbi of Viosk.' But she laughed, and turned to Hannah. 'Come, Chaya, help me set the table. We must eat and get to bed early. Tomorrow there is much to do.'

Hannah was silent through the dinner, fully expecting the food to fade away at her touch. She was surprised when it tasted real, not like dream food should have tasted, but she ate little of it, much to Gitl's annoyance.

'And how, my brother, do we put weight on those bones when she doesn't eat?'

Shmuel shrugged and didn't answer.

Hannah was silent as well when they led her into the room she apparently shared with Gitl. The whole household seemed so reasonable, she had to keep reminding herself it was all a stage setting in some kind of elaborate dream. Again and again she tried to pinch herself awake. All she got for it were sore spots on her arm.

At last, when she climbed into the hard little bed they insisted was hers, wearing a cotton nightshift that was, also, somehow her own, and Gitl had drawn up the puffy goosedown comforter over her, Hannah let out a long sigh. It was a lot like one of her mother's sighs, and she bit her lip remembering. If she tried hard, she thought she might even remember her mother's smell, a combination of face powder and Chanel Number Five.

'Poor little bird,' Gitl said, smoothing Hannah's hair and touching her cheek. *She* smelled of soap with an underlining of onion. 'Do you miss them still so much?'

Hannah nodded. 'My mother,' she said. 'And my father and . . .' The rest of the words didn't seem to come. Her head began to spin.

'Never mind, little Chaya, never mind,' Gitl said. 'Shmuel and I – we are your family now.'

5

HANNAH WOKE EARLY and the house was still pitch black and silent. Fearfully, she felt her way through the unfamiliar rooms in her nightgown and bare feet. The floor was cold underfoot. When she found the front door, she let out her breath slowly. *Now*, she thought, she'd open it and be back home. *Please. Please.*

Cautiously she pulled on the door and stared out.

Dawn was just beginning beyond the rim of the field. A thin strand of light spun out along the horizon between earth and sky. A rooster crowed his wake-up call into the clear air. *A-doo, a-doo* echoed back.

That was when she remembered the dream: she had been at a Seder, surrounded by familiar faces, and for some reason she hated being there. The sweet wine, the bitter herbs, she could almost taste them. She heard her aunt's voice singing the 'Dayenu' as if from miles away. Suddenly a terrible longing for all the people in the dream overcame her and she moaned softly.

'So you could not sleep either.' Shmuel's voice, deep and rumbling, came from the dark behind her. 'Getting married is the most frightening thing in the world, I think. But surely my marriage is not what kept you awake. Did you have another bad dream, Chaya? I worry about you and your dreams. A girl's dreams, like her life, should be sweet and filled with honey.'

She nodded slowly, then turned. She could see nothing in the black room. As if sensing that, Shmuel came over to stand by her side in the doorway. He was fully dressed and smoking a pipe. The curls of smoke feathered out into the open air, spreading themselves thinner and thinner, until at last they were gone.

'Do you think it strange, little Chaya, that I – Shmuel Abramowicz – with an arm like a tree and, as Gitl says, a head like a stone, should be afraid of getting married?' He flexed his left arm at her and grinned, but above the grin his eyes seemed troubled.

'Being married might be scary,' Hannah agreed tentatively.

'*Being* married does not bother me,' Shmuel said. But *getting* married – that frightens me!'

Not sure she understood the difference, Hannah hesitated. 'Maybe . . .' She took a deep breath and hurried on. 'Maybe there's something everyone is afraid of. With you it's getting married. With me it's shots.'

'Shots?'

'Shots. You know. Needles?' She jabbed her right finger into her left arm to demonstrate.

He smiled and nodded. 'You were very sick. I understand.'

'*Chaya* was sick, not me.'

He continued smiling, as if humoring her.

Hannah drew in a deep breath and sighed. 'My mother is afraid of snakes,' she said at last.

'There are not many snakes in Lublin!' Shmuel chuckled.

'I'm not from Lublin,' Hannah said 'I'm from New Rochelle. And I'm not Chaya, I'm Hannah.' When Shmuel's eyebrows rose up and lines furrowed his brow, he looked so fierce Hannah moved back a step. 'Of course,' she said quickly, 'there aren't many snakes in New Rochelle either. And Chaya *is* my Hebrew name, not Chanah, because of a friend of Aunt Eva's. And . . .'

'Lublin is a big place, I am sure,' Shmuel said, scratching his beard, with a gathering urgency. 'And surely I am not familiar with every avenue and street, having been there only twice in my life.'

'New Rochelle is not in Lublin, wherever that is. It's a city all its own,' Hannah cried.

'Since when is a street a city?'

Hannah could feel her voice getting louder, like Aaron's when he was scared, and a panic feeling was gripping her chest. 'New Rochelle is, too, a city. It's in New York.'

'Nu?'

Suddenly remembering Gitl's boyfriend Avrom, she shouted, 'In America!'

'And Krakow is in Siberia. I get it. A joke to help me forget about my marriage fears.' He laughed. 'Lublin in America and Krakow in Siberia. Though dear Gitl would say it most certainly is that far to both of them.' He reached out and patted Hannah on the head.

31

'What a strange little bird you are indeed, who has found her way into our nest. Gitl is right. But come, my little Americanisher, whose Yiddish is pure Lublinese, let us feed Hopel and Popel and discuss world geography some other time. Lublin in America, Krakow in Siberia.' He chuckled again as he held out a cloak for her and a pair of ugly black tie shoes.

Seeing that he was not taking her seriously, Hannah decided there was nothing else to do but go along. She took the clothes. The ugly shoes fitted perfectly. *Too* perfectly. She shivered, then followed him out to the barn, where they fed hay to the work horses, Popel and Hopel, in companionable silence.

Hoping for a big breakfast, Hannah was disappointed when all Gitl put on the table was a jug of milk, black coffee, and a loaf of dark bread.

'No cereal?' Hannah asked. 'No doughnuts? No white bread for toast?'

'White bread? So that is what one eats in Lublin. White bread is for rich folk, not for farmers.' Shmuel laughed. 'But yesterday you would eat nothing. Nothing at all. And today you want white bread. It is an improvement, I think. From nothing to Lublin white bread. Ah, but then I forget, you are not from Lublin, you are from Rochelle.'

'*New* Rochelle.'

'And where is Old Rochelle?' Gitl asked.

'There isn't any,' Hannah said, shaking her head. What was the point in arguing with dream people, who mixed you up. Anyway, she was starving, even if it *was* a dream. She reached for the milk pitcher and poured herself a glass of milk, took a swallow, and choked. It tasted awful. She looked into her glass. 'It's got *things* floating in it,' she said.

'What things?' Gitl looked.

'There.'

'That is not *things*. That is the cream. You have no cream in the milk in Lublin?'

'Rochelle,' said Shmuel.

'*New* Rochelle,' Hannah insisted.

'Old, new – what does it matter?' asked Gitl.

'But if there is no Old Rochelle, how can there be a New?' Shmuel mused out loud. 'Perhaps there is a Rochelle all alone, though the child does not know it.'

'*Pilpul!*' Gitl said. 'Men love to pursue questions without answers merely for the sake of arguing. It is what they do best. Ignore him, Chaya, a rabbi he is not.'

Hannah nodded and, noticing Shmuel wasn't eating, tried to pass him the pitcher of milk, but he waved it away.

'We do not follow all the old customs, Gitl and I, alone here and so far from the village. But I think it is not bad to hold to some of the traditions, like the groom's wedding fast.'

Gitl snorted. 'Especially if your stomach is nervous.'

'Me? Nervous? And what do I have to be nervous about?' Shmuel winked at Hannah as if binding her to silence.

'I heard you tossing and turning all night, Mr. I'm-

33

not-nervous. And I heard how early you got up this morning, even before the rooster crowed. Even before the spring sun.'

Shmuel seemed about to answer her back when there was a loud knock at the door.

Hannah jumped at the unexpected knock, then a small hope suddenly warmed her. Maybe the knock was some kind of signal that the dream, the strange play, was over. Maybe it was her mother or her father or Aunt Eva standing out there. She started to rise, but Gitl got up first and went to the door. When she opened it, the door framed a man with shoulders as wide as the door itself, wiry red hair, and a bushy red beard.

'Good morning, Yitzchak,' Shmuel called out.

Yitzchak greeted Shmuel in return, but he kept his eyes on Gitl, who gave him no more than a grunt in way of greeting.

'Have some coffee, Yitzchak. It is a long way through the forest from the shtetl to here, and even longer to Fayge's village,' Shmuel said, gesturing expansively with his hand. 'And have you heard about our little niece, Chaya?'

'*Little* is what I have heard, but what you have here is no *little* girl. She is a young lady,' Yitzchak said, grinning at her. 'And you are feeling better? I see good color in your cheeks.'

Hannah looked down at the table, embarrassed by the butcher's compliments, and Gitl reached over in front of her and took the coffeepot up, placing it down again with a solid *thwack* in front of Yitzchak.

34

Taking the pot up eagerly, Yitzchak poured himself a cupful that slopped over the rim.

Gitl made a small snick of annoyance between her teeth and wiped up the spill with the edge of her apron.

Almost shyly, Yitzchak smiled up at her, took a deep drink of coffee, then turned slowly to Shmuel. 'I have two cages of chickens outside, Shmuel. My wedding gift. Should I leave them or take them to Fayge's village with us?'

'Leave them. Leave them, Yitzchak,' Shmuel said. 'With our great thanks. After all, Fayge and I will be returning here for the wedding night and she will see them then.'

'If she sees anything but your blue eyes, then she is a fool,' Gitl said. 'She should be counting your curls, not her gifts. We will load the chickens in the wagon with the other wedding gifts. Those *schnorrers* in Viosk will not think we do not honor our own.'

Shmuel laughed. 'Gitl and Chaya will stay the night with Fayge's people and come back home in the morning. It would not do . . . the walls are thin . . .' He actually blushed, and Gitl put her hand on his shoulder.

'Do not say it step by step in front of the child,' she said.

'I did no such thing, Gitl. I was careful. I said only that the walls are thin. And so they are.'

'He meant no disrespect,' Yitzchak added quickly.

'Hush, Yitzchak the butcher. Do not tell me in my house what is and what is not.' Gitl's eyes sparked.

Hannah interrupted. 'But I know what a wedding

night is.'

All three stared at her and Yitzchak laughed nervously.

'You see,' he said, 'I told you she was a young woman.'

'You said a young *lady* and a lady is what she is not if she knows such things,' Gitl said.

'It's on "General Hospital",' Hannah began.

Gitl turned to Hannah and shook her head. 'So in Lublin the hospitals tell you about these things. Then I do not think much of hospitals. And I think even less of Lublin. You know so much, my little *yeshiva bocher*, telling you anything more is carrying straw to Egypt. Ah!' She threw her hands up in the air and spun around to face Yitzchak. 'And you – you finish your coffee. Look how the morning flies, and we sit here gabbling about wedding nights, which will be here soon enough. I have still to clean the house. I will not have Fayge coming here, fresh from her father's house where there is a serving girl to clean, and think me and all in this shtetl slovens. We have to leave before noon.'

'That is why I came early, Gitl, so I might help. My children, too.' Yitzchak stood, the coffee cup still in his hand.

'The children – oy. And where did you leave them? Outside in cages like the chickens?' She clicked her tongue and went to the door. Opening it, she waved her hand in greeting. 'Reuven, Tzipporah, come in.'

Two little blond-haired children, no more three or four years old, suddenly appeared in the doorway, silently holding hands.

'Go, sit at the table with my niece Chaya, the young lady over there,' Gitl said. 'She will give you milk with *things* in it and tell you stories of places called *New* this and *Old* that. Then you can go outside with her and feed the horses and chickens.'

'The horses are fed,' Shmuel said. 'The chickens I will tend to myself, with Yitzchak and the children. Chaya can help you here in the house. There is enough to do.'

Yitzchak's massive hands made surprisingly dainty circles in the air. 'My children and I will take care of the animals. Tzipporah is wonderful about collecting eggs. A real specialist. And Reuven knows just when to shoo them off the nest.' He smiled down at his children, who looked up at him adoringly. 'We are sorry if we disturbed you. We thought we would come over early and, in that way, help.'

'Help!' Gitl sniffed, but she smiled at the children.

No sooner had Yitzchak disappeared outside with Reuven and Tzipporah than Shmuel laughed out loud. 'I swear, Gitl, that man is already henpecked and not even married to you yet.'

'He is a monster,' Gitl murmured. 'Imagine leaving those sweet, motherless children outside like chickens in cages.' She began to swipe at the table furiously with a wet rag.

'I thought he was nice,' Hannah ventured.

'*Nice!*' Gitl's voice rose. 'But then you know so much about raising motherless children, too, I suppose.'

Hannah closed her mouth. Argument was useless. Instead, she began to clear away the dishes with silent efficiency and seemed to be the only one who was surprised that she was helping.

6

'COME, IT IS TIME TO GET DRESSED,' Gitl said.

Dressed! Hannah looked down at the flowered smock she had on, the same awful thing she'd been wearing the night before. Anything would be better. It looked like one of her grandmother's house dresses, shapeless, with faded roses. Following Gitl into the bedroom, she paused only a moment, wondering without much hope if the door would transport her back to the Bronx. But when she passed through, the small, dark bedroom was still solidly itself. What was dream and what was real were getting harder and harder to distinguish.

'What should I wear, Gitl?' The woman's name came easily now to her tongue. Hannah wasn't even sure where the closet was that held her clothes, her *real* clothes. The bedroom she and Gitl had shared had only one door, which led back into the main living-dining room. There were two small beds in it with wooden chests at the foot of each, and a large standing wardrobe. Between the two beds was a washstand with a stoneware pitcher and bowl. She had already discovered, to her horror, that the bathroom was a privy outside the house, and it had no light for night visits.

'You will wear the dress I wore as a child for Shmuel's Bar Mitzvah. He was so handsome – and so nervous. Just like today. It is too bad that your wonderful clothes from Lublin had to be burned along with your bedding, but the doctors said they carried the disease. As you arrived just two days ago, there was no time to make you anything else. But do not worry, Chaya, I will make you new clothes before winter comes.'

While Hannah stood in the center of the room, wondering which chest she should try first, Gitl went to the standing wardrobe, opened it, and pulled out a dark blue sailor-suit dress with white piping at the sleeves and neck, and a blue sash belt. It was the ugliest thing Hannah had ever seen. And babyish.

'Lovely,' Gitl said. 'Nicer than anything any of the girls in our shtetl or Fayge's have. All the other girls will be jealous.'

'Jealous? Of that?' Hannah was momentarily speechless, then muttered under her breath, 'It's a rag, a *shmatte*.'

Gitl made a sound of disgust. 'In Lublin it may be a *shmatte*. But here it is fit for a princess. Even Fayge in her wedding dress will not be as beautiful. Now, young lady, no more nonsense. Perhaps we have been babying you too long, Miss I-know-what-a-wedding-night-is.'

Hannah's face must have shown its instant apology through burning cheeks, for Gitl came over immedi-

40

ately and put her arm around Hannah. 'There, there, child, forgive me. I am crazy with all this wedding business, and my tongue is sometimes quicker than my heart. Put on the dress. Perhaps it is, after all, a little out of fashion, but then so are we here in our shtetl. And you are not in Lublin now.'

She paused for a moment as if waiting for Hannah's reply. When there was none, she went on as before. 'Try on the stockings and shoes. I only used them for *shul* and for the photographer. And then I grew, in one year, too big for them. They still have plenty of wear left and I think they will fit you nicely. I was just your size at fifteen. At sixteen I was a giant! Then I will do your hair for you and everything will look fine, you will see.'

Hannah pulled the dress on. It fitted her perfectly in the bodice and the sleeves, but came down way over her knees. Gitl didn't seem to see anything wrong with that. The stockings were a heavy skin-colored cotton that came halfway up her thighs, the shoes shiny black mary janes. Shaking her head, Hannah put them on as well. If she pretended she was going to a Halloween party, the outfit would be bearable.

Gitl braided her hair into two tight plaits, then held up a pair of blue velvet ribbons. 'These I was saving for my own wedding night about which you know so much.' This time her voice held a hint of laughter. 'But who would marry that monster Yitzchak, who leaves his precious children outside like yard goods? Besides, the ribbons will look beautiful in your brown hair.' She tied them around the ends of the plaits, then pinned the plaits on top of Hannah's head like a crown. 'There! Look!' She pushed Hannah toward a mirror that hung on the wall.

Hannah looked. Gone were her braces. Gone was the light coral lipstick her mother had allowed her to wear to the Seder. The girl who stared back had the same heart-shaped face, the same slightly crooked smile, the same brown hair, the same gray eyes as Hannah Stern of New Rochelle, New York, in America. But there was something old-fashioned and unfamiliar about this Chaya Abramowicz, something haunting, like one of the old photographs on Grandma Belle's grand piano. Photographs of Grandma's family but none of Grandpa Will's, because, Aunt Eva had once explained, no photographs had been saved in the death camps. 'We are our own photos. Those pictures are engraved only in our memories. When we are gone, they are gone.'

Hannah smiled awkwardly at her reflection and turned away.

By noon, half the shtetl was gathered outside their door, laughing and trading stories so loudly the chickens hid in the barn, refusing to come out even when three little boys in short pants and *yarmulkes* tried to coax them with corn.

Hannah felt a lot like the chickens, nervous about all the loud, strange men and the laughing, chattering women. She, too, would have hidden in the barn if she could. Sensing Hannah's timidity, Gitl kept her close as she greeted everyone by name, thanking them for the gifts as if she were the bride herself.

Looking surprisingly beautiful in a dark green dress with a broad white lace collar, Gitl made sure all the tributes were piled onto two wagons: crocks of butter, lengths of cloth, a white lace tablecloth, wooden bowls, and a pair of truly ugly silver candlesticks that Shmuel announced had been sent over by the *rendar* himself. Even the cages of chickens went into the wagons, one in each. Gitl kept rearranging the gifts, making them seem to be twice as numerous, saying again, 'Those *schnorrers* in Viosk will know we honor our own.'

Near the barn, Shmuel and the other men stood smoking and laughing at one joke after another. When Gitl disappeared inside for a moment, Hannah thought she'd stand next to Shmuel, since she really knew no one else. But when she got close, Yitzchak shooed her away as if she were one of the chickens, waving his massive hands at her and saying, 'Men-talk is not for young ladies.'

Embarrassed at being singled out that way, Hannah spun around, right into the arms of a girl her own age, who looked at her with great, startled green eyes. Hannah was so relieved to see another girl, she almost cried out.

'So – you are Lublin Chaya,' the girl said, her voice catching strangely in mid-sentence. Before Hannah could deny it, the girl had threaded her arm through Hannah's, calling out to a knot of girls who were standing by a newly arrived wagon. 'I have found her, Lublin Chaya.'

They came over at a run, hair ribbons flying.

'You see, we have all been waiting to meet you' the startled-looking girl explained, the breathiness in her voice more pronounced. 'Ever since we heard you were coming. Imagine, someone from Lublin living in our shtetl. But Tante Gitl is so fierce. Do you know my father calls her Gitl the Bear?'

'My father, too,' one of the other girls said.

'She said we could not meet you until you had rested because you had been so seriously ill. Almost died, she said.' The startled girl pulled each statement out as if it were a rare gift to be examined, breathing deeply after every sentence. 'Ten weeks in the hospital, and no one here knowing. But she promised we would meet you. At the wedding. And here you are.'

Hannah pulled a smile across her face in greeting. At least the dream – or whatever it was – would be more interesting with girls her own age in it.

'Now let me introduce you,' the breathless girl said. 'This is Shifre, Esther, and Yente – but we call *her* the Cossack!'

They each bobbed a head in turn.

'And I,' she drew in a deep, heavy breath, 'I am Rachel. I am going to be your best friend.'

'I already have a best friend,' Hannah said. 'At home. Her name is Rosemary.'

'What kind of a name is Rosemary?' asked one of the girls. Hannah thought it might have been Shifre.

'It is a goyish name,' Rachel said at once. 'Do you mean to say your best friend is not a Jew?'

'As a matter of fact, she's Catholic,' Hannah said.

'As if that matters.'

'As if that matters!' The girls were clearly shocked, and Esther added, 'My father will not let me even *talk* to a goy.'

'Esther, your father will not let you talk to someone from Viosk,' said Rachel.

'Well, I am going to talk to someone from Viosk today!' Esther answered. 'After I talk to Lublin Chaya.'

Hannah turned to Rachel, shaking her head slowly. 'You can be my second-best friend, Rachel. My first-best here.' It seemed somehow important to keep the two worlds separate. She was sure Rosemary would understand.

The girls all smiled at her, waiting for something else, and Hannah could not figure out what. Trying to memorize their faces, to distinguish them, she saw that Shifre had a pale freckled face and eyelashes so light they could not be seen. It made her eyes look shifty. *Shifre – shifty*. She could remember that. And Esther was plump with rosy cheeks and a mouth that seemed to rest in a pout. She was round like an Easter egg. *Esther – Easter*. The third girl, the Cossack Yente, had a ferrety face, sharp in chin and nose, and a yellowish complexion. *Yente – yellow*. It was a special way of remembering Aunt Eva had taught her. It worked so well, she got *A*s in school using it. And Rachel was just Rachel. Her second-best friend, first here in the shtetl, in the dream.

'So,' Rachel said, interrupting her thoughts, 'tell us about Lublin.'

Hannah realized it would be as useless telling them she lived in New Rochelle as it had been trying to convince Gitl and Shmuel. The truth was, she was beginning to wonder herself whether she was Hannah and Chaya was the dream or if she was Chaya and Hannah was some kind of *mishigaas*, some craziness in her mind from the sickness. Yet there were all those memories – of house and school and Seder; of Mother and Father and Aaron and Aunt Eva and the rest. She couldn't have made them all up. Unless she was a genius. Or crazy. Or both.

She had no choice. 'In Lublin,' she began, thinking of New Rochelle, 'I live in a house that has eight rooms and the toilets are *inside* the house. One upstairs and one downstairs.'

'*In* the house?' Rachel let it out in a single breath.

'Imagine,' said Yente, 'your parents must have been fabulously wealthy. Richer than Yitzchak the butcher. As rich, almost, as the *rendar* himself.'

'The *rendar*'s house has twelve rooms,' Rachel said.

'Thirteen,' Yente corrected. 'My mother's sister is his housekeeper.' Her sharp nosed twitched as she talked.

'Your mother's sister cannot count,' said Rachel. 'She thinks there are thirteen eggs in a dozen.'

'She thinks there are nine days of Chanukah,' added Shifre.

'She thinks there are five fingers on a hand,' Esther put in dreamily.

'Idiot, there *are* five fingers on a hand,' Rachel said to Esther.

'I know that.'

'Never mind her,' Rachel confided to Hannah. 'She never understands a joke. Now, Chaya, tell us more.'

'More,' Hannah said, trying to think what might interest them. 'Well, during the week I go to school, but on the weekends I go with Rosemary to the mall and . . .'

'School, too!' Esther said with a sigh. 'Only boys are allowed to go to school here. I always wanted to go.'

'You *want* to go?' Hannah was shocked. 'No one I know does. We can't wait for the weekends. That's when we can have fun, go shopping, and . . .'

It was the girls' turn to be shocked. 'Shopping? On the Sabbath?' Rachel asked.

Esther was still thinking about the school. 'I heard once about a girl who disguised herself as a boy and went into a *yeshivah* to study Torah. I do not believe it.'

'I know that story.' Hannah's voice rose in excitement. It's called *Yentl* and stars Barbra Streisand in the movie. She chops off her hair and . . .'

'Chops off her hair!' Appalled, Shifre put her hands up to her own pale braids. 'And not married?'

'We have never seen a movie,' said Esther. 'But I have heard of them.'

'Never mind from movies,' Rachel said sternly, the breathiness gone from her voice for once. 'And no more interruptions. Tell us the story of this Yentl, Chaya. From the beginning.'

7

Stories seemed to tumble out of Hannah's mouth, reruns of all the movies and books she could think of. She told the girls about *Yentl* and then about *Conan the Barbarian* with equal vigor; about *Star Wars*, which confused them; and *Fiddler on the Roof*, which did not. She told them the plot of *Little Women* in ten minutes, a miracle of compression, especially since her book report had been seven typed pages.

She mesmerized them with her tellings. After the first one, which they had interrupted every third sentence with questions, they were an attentive audience, and silent except for their frequent loud sighs and Esther's nervous laughter at all the wrong moments.

Rachel cried at the end of *Yentl*, when Hannah described Barbra Streisand bravely sailing off to America alone. And all four had tears running down their cheeks when Beth died in *Little Women*. Hannah wondered at this strange power she held in her mouth. It was true Aaron had always liked her stories. So did Rosemary, but as her best friend she had to. And the

Brodie twins, whom she'd only started to babysit, could usually be kept quiet with a tale. But she'd never had such a large, appreciative audience before.

Walking through the woods behind the wagons, the girls kept jostling one another for the place of honor by Hannah's side. Hannah wondered about *that* most of all. In New Rochelle, except for Rosemary and two other friends, who had all been together since first grade, she was not very popular. There was even one clique of girls – Rosemary called them 'the Snubs' – who never spoke to her, though three were in her Hebrew class and one was actually Rosemary's cousin. She remembered vividly standing with Rosemary at the school's water fountain, giggling and splashing each other. The Snubs came over and called them babies just when Jordan Mandel went by. He'd laughed at them and Hannah had thought she'd die on the spot. Yet here, wherever *here* was, she was suddenly the most popular girl on the block. Except there wasn't any block. She realized that she couldn't have made up that powerful memory. She *was* Hannah. But these girls, who were hanging on her every word, believed she was Chaya. And it was great to be so popular. She wasn't going to spoil it by trying to convince them she really was someone else.

'So let me tell you about *The Wizard of Oz*,' she said. She couldn't remember which was the movie and which was the book. Shrugging her shoulders, she began a strange mixture of the two, speeding along until the line 'Gosh, Toto, this sure doesn't look like Kansas.'

'What is Kansas?' Rachel asked.

Just then Gitl dropped back and listened to them. Hannah was afraid she would interrupt them or make her ride in the wagon. But all Gitl said was 'Kansas, it is in America. Near New Rochelle.' Then she walked away, laughing.

As they wound on through the forest, Hannah guessed everybody from the shtetl was there. The littlest children and some of the older women rode in the open wagons, but everyone else walked. Sunlight filtered through the canopy of large trees, spotlighting the forest. *It was even more magical than the forest in Oz*, Hannah thought. When she stopped for a moment to take it all in, the girls complained.

'Go on, go on,' Shifre said. 'What happened next?'

Putting her arm around Hannah's waist, Rachel smiled. 'Let her be. She is only catching her breath.'

'*You* are the one who has trouble catching her breath,' said Yente the Cossack. She wrinkled her long nose. 'But Chaya has plenty of breath. Shifre is right. What happened next to this Dorothy Gale?'

Hannah was in the middle of a muddled version of *Hansel and Gretel*, having temporarily run out of movies and books and fallen back on the nursery tales she told Aaron or the Brodie twins, when her attention was arrested by a high, thin, musical wail. She stopped in mid-sentence.

The others heard it at the same time and Yente clapped her hands.

'The *klezmer!*' she cried out. 'We're almost there.'

50

She had been holding Hannah's arm, but pulled away half a step to look longingly toward the front of the line.

For a moment, Hannah was almost annoyed at having her audience distracted. 'Don't you want to hear any more?' she asked.

'Never mind her, Chaya,' Rachel said smoothly. 'How are you to guess Yente knows songs like you know stories? She will leave the dinner table, even, at the sound of a clarinet. So ignore her and finish about this witch. Does she push Gretel in the oven or not?'

But the mood was broken and a new mood took over the villagers as the sound from the clarinet reached them. The pace of the walk, which had become leisurely, quickened. Even the horses picked up their step. The constant chatter stopped. Everyone seemed to be straining to listen.

Then another instrument joined in. It took a moment for Hannah to realize that the second was a violin. It certainly wasn't like the one she had labored on in Suzuki class so long and with so little result. This violin had a piercing, insistent sweetness of tone, almost like a baby crying.

The wagons came to a halt as the *klezmer* band came around a bend in the forest path. Hannah saw that there were three musicians in all: the clarinet, the violin, and an accordion. The music was fast and full of a wild energy.

The band members strode down the line of villagers. Behind them came Shmuel, dancing with abandon, his hands above his head and his black hair a dark halo around it. Yitzchak followed him, big hands clapping in rhythm. Other men soon joined them. Laughing and shouting encouragement, the women watched from the side. Then they began to sing.

'Sing, Chaya!' Shmuel called as he danced by her. 'Sing!'

'I don't know the words,' she called back. But even as she said it, she found herself singing, the words stumbling out as if her mouth remembered what her mind did not, as if her mouth belonged to Chaya, her head to Hannah. She began to clap madly in rhythm until the tune came to an abrupt end.

'Look,' Rachel cried above the noise, the breathiness back in her voice, 'they have even brought a *badchan*. Fayge's father must have a lot of money.'

'Or an only daughter,' Esther added.

'Then why is she marrying Shmuel?' Shifre blurted out. Looking at Hannah apologetically, she added, 'I mean he is handsome but he is not so rich or so learned. And you know about Rabbi Boruch . . .'

'They say . . . ,' Rachel began, and the girls bent closer to her as her breath gave out, '. . . they say that Fayge is his favorite and always gets her way. They say she saw Shmuel and fell in love.'

'In love.' The girls breathed the words in rhythm.

'So?' Hannah was puzzled. 'So they fell in love.'

'So – it may happen in Lublin that a Jewish girl marries for love,' said Shifre. 'But here in the country, we still marry the one our parents pick out with the *shadchan*, the marriage broker. '

'Even today?' Hannah asked, not sure when *today*

was.

'Even today,' they all said together.

Hannah turned to look at the man Rachel had pointed out as the *badchan*. She wondered who he was. The word seemed to have no easy translation in her head. As she watched, the tall, skinny man circulated from group to group. Each knot of people he left was laughing uproariously. Maybe he was some sort of comedian.

When the *badchan* got to the girls, he squatted down in front of them. He was so tall, even squatting, he towered a full head above Rachel, who was the smallest of them. Then he began in a sing-song manner to rhyme about each one in turn. When he got to Hannah, he pointed his finger at her and sang:

Pretty girl, with faraway eyes,
Why do you look with such surprise?
How did you get to be so wise,
Old girl in young-girl disguise.

'That is you, Chaya!' Gitl cried out from behind them. 'What a fine *badchan*.'

Without taking his eyes off Hannah, the *badchan* said, 'So, your name is Chaya, which is to say, *life*. A strong name for a strange time, child. Be good *life* and long *life* to your friends, young-old Chaya.' He stood up slowly, unfolding like some kind of long-legged bird, and danced away to the next group of villagers.

'Strange,' Hannah remarked to no one in particular.

'Well, that is what he is hired to be,' Rachel said. 'Strange and mysterious and to make up rhymes, sing songs, tell fortunes. He said I looked startled by life, Chaya. Do you think so?' She put her arm through Hannah's.

Hannah shrugged, but she wasn't really thinking about what Rachel said. She was watching the *badchan*. He reminded her of something or someone, but she couldn't think what. Then, when he tipped his hat to one of the old women on the wagons, it came to her. He was like a court jester. Only instead of wearing one of those colorful caps with bells, he wore a black hat like the other men, and the bottom of his coat danced along with his every move.

The idea of a Jewish jester so tickled her, she began to laugh out loud. Without even knowing the joke, the other girls joined in.

8

THE FOREST WAS NOW boiling with people, for the Viosk villagers had come behind the *klezmer* to greet Shmuel and his friends. Hannah hung back. More people meant more greetings and more excuses. It was worse than any family party at home.

At home! The skin on her face suddenly felt stretched tight across her cheekbones and her eyes began to prickle with tears. *Where* was *her home?* She forced herself to recall the house in New Rochelle with its borders of flowers and the flagstone walk. But the image seemed to be fading, especially when compared with the forest full of villagers and the tiny house and horse barn she'd left just hours before.

A hand on her arm riveted her to the moment.

'Come, Chaya,' Gitl said. 'Come and meet your new aunt-to-be.' Pulling Hannah past the noisy celebrants, Gitl led her to the one wagon facing the rest, where the men were busy at work encouraging the two strong workhorses to turn around.

On that wagon sat two people, one an older man dressed all in black, with a white prayer shawl across his shoulders, a book in his lap. The other was one of the most beautiful women Hannah had ever seen, like a movie star. She was all in white, with an elegantly beaded headdress capping her hair. That hair was jet black, so black that it didn't even have lighter highlights, and electric with curls spilling over her shoulders. There were gold rings on her fingers and gold dangling from her ears. She had a strong nose and a fierce, piercing look, like a bird of prey

'Fayge,' Gitl said, 'this is my niece, Chaya.'

Hannah wondered how, with all the noise and excitement, Fayge even heard Gitl's introduction. But she looked down from the wagon, those eagle eyes staring. Then she smiled, not at all fiercely, but even shyly.

'The Lubliner. Come, you must be exhausted, walking all this way after having been so sick. Shmuel would never forgive me if I did not let you ride. And what a pretty dress. You put us all to shame.' She leaned down and offered her hand.

'I will not say I told you so,' Gitl whispered into Hannah's ear, 'but I did.'

As if in a dream, Hannah reached up for Fayge's hand. She expected a princess's hand, small, fine-boned, soft. But Fayge's hand was large and strong, with calluses in the palm. When she was up by Fayge's side, she could smell a scent on her hair and dress, like roses and wood shavings after a long rain.

'Now,' Fayge said, turning toward her and smiling broadly. 'Tell me all about Lublin.'

The bride's wagon was turned around at last, and the procession started up again. This time the *klezmer* was behind, far back at the end of the line of villagers. Hannah's new friends danced by the wagon's side, hands joined, singing:

Who asked you to get married?
Who asked you to be buried alive?
You know that no one forced you,
You took this madness on yourself.

'I always hated the "Sherele",' Fayge said. 'Such a gloomy song for so glorious an event.'

'What's the "Sherele"?' Hannah asked.

'The wedding dance your friends are doing. You do not play such games in Lublin? Perhaps you are smarter than we.'

Hannah looked down at the girls. Some younger girls had joined them and the line was twisting and turning to the rhythm of the song. 'New Rochelle,' she murmured, though this time it was more a prayer than a statement.

Fayge didn't seem to hear. 'Oh, Chaya, never mind the "Sherele." We will sing and dance other things all-night long. The grandmothers will dance the "Bobbe Tants" – well, Shmuel's grandmother is gone, may she rest in peace. But Gitl can dance with my grandmother. You should see my grandmother, so light and quick. And you, too, Chaya, you will dance. Oh, only if you are feeling well enough. We will have great fun. You will see.' She patted Hannah's hand.

The wagon bumped along the road, swaying from side to side. Hannah wished she could get down and looked longingly at the ground.

'What is it, Chayaleh?' Fayge asked.

'Is it much longer?'

'Around one more big bend and we will be there. At my village. At Viosk. Would you believe it? My village for but a few more hours and then my village no more. *And* would you guess that as excited as I am about marrying my beloved Shmuel, a part of me is also afraid?'

Hannah laughed out loud. 'Shmuel said the same thing this morning.'

'Did he? Did he?' Fayge's eyes lit up and suddenly she looked very young, not that much older than Hannah. 'Tell me exactly what he said.'

Hannah closed her eyes, trying to remember. 'He said . . . he said . . .'

'Yes?'

'He said he wasn't afraid of *being* married, only of *getting* married.'

Reb Boruch cleared his throat loudly.

'Oh, Chaya,' Fayge said, ignoring her father, 'thank you for telling me that.' She gave Hannah a hug. 'We are going to be such friends, you and I. Best friends. Life will be good to us forever and ever, I know.'

The wagon made a wide turn around the bend in the path, the horses straining mightily. One blew out its nostrils, a loud huffing. Ahead, where the path widened out, was a meadow and beyond it a town.

Hannah called over her shoulder to the dancing girls, 'We're here,' the words springing easily to her mouth. The girls dropped hands and stared down the path.

When Hannah looked up again, she could see Viosk laid out at the far end of the meadow, picture-postcard pretty. Small houses nestled in a line, and the larger buildings, none higher than three stories, stood behind, like mothers with their children.

As the horses pulled them closer, Hannah could distinguish a central open market with stalls, surrounded by stores. There was a pharmacy topped by a large black sign, a barbershop with its familiar peppermint stick, a glass-fronted tavern, and a dozen other shops. In the middle of the market, a tall wooden pole supported a bell. Behind the open market was a towering wooden building with four separate roofed sections and fenced-in courtyards. The dominant color was brown: brown wooden buildings, brown sandy streets, as if it were a faded photograph. Yet it was real.

'Papa,' Fayge said, turning to him, 'what are those automobiles and trucks doing in front of the *shul*?' She pointed to one of the big buildings. 'Is it another surprise for the wedding? Oh, Papa!' She gave him a hug, and his normally dour face lit up.

Hannah looked where Fayge was pointing. In the middle of the brown landscape, like a dark stain, were three black old-fashioned cars and twelve army trucks strung out behind. She gave an involuntary shudder. They reminded her of something; she couldn't think what.

Fayge's father cleared his throat and closed the book on his lap. 'I do not make surprises,' he said gruffly. 'Only my children make surprises.'

'Then what are those automobiles and trucks doing

in front of our *shul*?' Fayge asked.

The wagon continued its slow side-to-side pace toward the town, but behind it the villagers grew silent as one by one they noticed what sat in front of the synagogue.

Shmuel hurried forward. Putting his hand on the wagon, close to Fayge's hand but not quite touching it, he addressed her father formally.

'Reb Boruch, excuse me,' Shmuel said, 'but do you know just what it is that lies ahead?'

'I am not a fortune teller nor yet a *badchan*,' Reb Boruch said. 'It is to God you must address such questions.'

Just then the door of the first car opened and a man in a black uniform with high black boots stepped out. He turned and opened the car's back door. Another man, similarly dressed, unfolded himself from the seat. The medals on his chest caught the light from the spring sun, sending undecipherable signals across the market to them.

Somehow the *badchan* materialized in front of the wagon. He pointed to the man with the medals and cried out, 'I see the *malach ha-mavis*. I see the Angel of Death.'

Hannah felt the breath catch in her throat. *Malach ha-mavis*. That was her grandfather's phrase, the one he had shouted at her when she drew the long number on her arm. *Angel of death*. Slowly, carefully, she turned to Shmuel, afraid to move too quickly, afraid she might not be quick enough. 'Please, Shmuel, what year is it? Please.'

60

He laughed, but there was little brightness in it. 'They do not have the same year in Lublin?'

'Please.'

Fayge put her hand on Hannah's. 'Silly child,' she said, her voice curiously hushed, 'It is 5701.'

'5701? But this can't be the future,' Hannah said. 'It doesn't look like the future. You don't have movies or new cars or . . .' Her voice was hoarse.

'She has been this way ever since she arrived, Fayge,' Shmuel said, shaking his head. 'Sometimes she is lucid, other times she talks of Rochelles and needles and snakes.' He tapped his finger to his forehead. 'It is the sickness, I think. And the loss of her parents. Now she talks of the future.'

Reb Boruch cleared his throat. 'I think the child means *loym kristlichen luach*, according to the Christian calendar.'

'They do not know from the Jewish calendar in Lublin?' Fayge asked.

'1942. It is several days before Passover,' the *badchan* said.

'*Before* Passover?' Hannah drew in a deep breath. And then, all of a sudden, she knew. She knew beyond any doubt where she was. She was not Hannah Stern of New Rochelle, at least not anymore, though she still had Hannah's memories. Those memories, at least, might serve as a warning.

'The men down there,' she cried out desperately, 'they're not wedding guests. They're Nazis. Nazis! Do you understand? They kill people. They killed – kill – will kill Jews. Hundreds of them. Thousands of them.

Six million of them! I know. Don't ask me how I know, I just do. We have to turn the wagons around. We have to run!'

Reb Boruch shook his head. 'There are not six million Jews in all of Poland, my child.'

'No, Rabbi, six million in Poland and Germany and Holland and France and . . .'

'My child, *such* a number.' He shook his head and smiled, but the corners of his mouth turned down instead of up. 'And as for running – where would we run to? God is everywhere. There will always be Nazis among us. No, my child, do not tremble before mere men. It is God before whom we must tremble. Only God. We will go ahead, just as we have planned. After all, this is our shtetl, not theirs, and there is still a wedding to be made.' He lifted his hand. On his signal, the wagons started up again across the last few yards to the market. As they moved closer, more men in dark uniforms got out of the cars and truck cabs. They made a perfect half circle in front of the synagogue doors, like a steel trap with gaping jaws ready to be sprung.

THE VILLAGERS GATHERED uneasily within the half-circle of soldiers and waited to be let into the *shul*. There was hardly any talking, but Yitzchak's young son, Reuven, began to whimper. To quiet him, Yitzchak lifted the boy onto his shoulders.

Rabbi Boruch, Shmuel, and another man Hannah did not know conferred hastily with the Nazi chief, the one with all the medals. They spoke in swift, hurried bursts of words that Hannah could not distinguish, but she could see Shmuel's fists clenching and unclenching behind his back. They were a violent punctuation to all those undistinguishable sentences, as if Shmuel wanted to shake his fist in the Nazi's face but didn't dare. At last the argument was done and Shmuel came over to them.

He spoke gently. 'They insist that we go with them in those trucks.'

'No!' Hannah protested in a whisper.

'Their argument is persuasive,' Shmuel answered, his thumb and forefinger pointed at her like a gun. 'They say all Jews are being resettled. It is government policy.'

'I heard that too,' Yitzchak added. 'Government policy. They have been settling villages closer to the big cities. I thought out here they would leave us alone.'

Another man argued, 'What does a goyish government have to do with us?'

'A kick in the face and a hand in the pocket,' said another.

'Wait, wait,' Shmuel said. His voice was soft but his face was grim. 'Remember those guns.'

Fayge moved silently into the protection of his arms. 'What about our wedding?' She meant it for his ears alone but Hannah was close enough to him to hear every plaintive syllable.

'We *will* be married, Fayge. Your father will marry us. Maybe not here, in your *shul*. Maybe not even under a wedding canopy.'

'Not under a canopy?' Fayge was shocked.

'We *will* be married, in God's sight,' Shmuel said adamantly. 'I promise you that nothing will keep us apart.'

'The Nazis will,' Hannah said suddenly. She could feel the rapid thudding of her heart as she spoke. 'They'll take you from here and put you in a concentration camp. Then they'll put you in gas ovens and kill you.' She could hear her voice rise in pitch; its intensity frightened her.

'Chaya!' Gitl said sharply, putting her fingers up to Hannah's lips and whispering hoarsely at her. 'Hush! The soldiers will hear.'

Turning in Shmuel's arms, Fayge stared at Hannah,

her beautiful face sharp, her eyes nearly all pupil. 'How can you talk like that? Your words will fly up to heaven and call down the Angel of Death, Lilith's bridegroom, with his poisoned sword.'

Gitl shook her finger at Fayge. 'Nonsense! You talk like one of the old women in the village – angels and poisoned swords. Why not flying chariots and the finger of the Lord? Chaya does no such thing. How could she? She is only a child, as you are no longer. She is a child with too much imagination and stories filling her head. She has just been recalled by a miracle from the doors of death. Shame, shame, Fayge, to make her into some kind of monster.'

Rachel interrupted. 'Tante Gitl, I think I know what Chaya is talking about. She told us a story this morning. About two children named . . .' She thought a moment. 'Yes, Hansel and Gitl.'

'Gretel,' Hannah corrected automatically.

'Yes, Gretel,' Rachel said. 'And there is a witch who shoves little boys into ovens and eats them.' She shuddered and drew a deep breath. 'A fairy tale.'

'The gas ovens I mean are no fairy tale,' Hannah said.

Gitl raised her chin, squinted her eyes and, ignoring Hannah, addressed Fayge directly. 'See, my almost sister-in-law, the child was just reciting a story. And surely we have more important things to worry about than *bobbe meinses*, tall tales.' Her hands went up and then back down to her skirt, where she wiped them twice.

'And what could be more important than such a

curse,' Fayge asked, adding slowly, 'my sister Gitl?'

Gitl smiled. 'Are your mother and grandmother not important? Where are they? Why have they not come out to greet us?'

Fayge looked around. 'Gitl, you are right. Where are they? And where is Tante Sarah and Tante Devorah and . . .' Her voice trailed off and she turned back to look at Shmuel. 'And all the rest, where are they?' Her hand twisted and twisted one gold earbob nervously.

Stony-faced, Shmuel wouldn't look down to meet her eyes. In a flat voice he said, 'The colonel informed us that they have been sent for resettlement already. We will meet them there.'

'You can't believe that!' Hannah cried.

'What else can we believe?' Shmuel asked. 'Gas ovens? Lilith's bridegroom? Poisoned swords? The Angel of Death?'

Just then Reb Boruch cleared his throat loudly and all the little knots of people who had been talking fell silent.

'My friends, my neighbors, my children,' he began, 'it seems we have no choice in this matter. The government has decreed that we are to be relocated for the duration of this war. This war in which we Jews take no part. So it is with governments.'

There was a murmur of assent from the men.

'My wife, my mother, my sisters – and all of yours – those who were waiting here in Viosk for our return from the forest, those who were getting ready for the wedding, they have been sent ahead. They have taken with them what clothing and household goods we shall need in the resettlement camp.'

'But what of *our* clothes and *our* goods,' called out Yitzchak, 'those of us who are not from Viosk?'

'We will share what we have,' said the rabbi. 'For are we not all neighbors and friends? Are we not all brothers and sisters in God's eye? Are we not . . .'

'All will be taken care of,' said the Nazi colonel, interrupting smoothly. 'You will want for nothing.'

'We wanted for nothing except to be left alone here in Viosk,' said a voice.

'Nevertheless,' the colonel continued, smiling, 'in this matter, *we* will make the ruling. When you get to your new homes, anyone who wants to work will be treated humanely. The tailor will sew, the shoemaker will have his last. And you will be happy among your own people, just as we will be happy you have followed the government's orders.'

'The snake smiles but it shows no teeth,' murmured the *badchan*. Hannah wondered if anyone else heard him.

Raising his hands, the rabbi began to speak. 'The colonel has assured me that some of his soldiers will remain billeted here to guard our stores and houses and schools from harm while we are gone. At my request, the soldiers will pay special attention to the *shul* to make sure the peasants do not desecrate it.'

'Better the fox to guard the hens and the wolves to guard the sheep,' the *badchan* said.

This time he was heard, and there were murmurs in the crowd. One man called out, 'But Reb Boruch, why would they billet soldiers here if they are needed elsewhere for the war?'

'Am I a general to answer such questions?' the rabbi asked. 'Am I the head of state? I only know that they have promised me this, so this I believe. They say the war is almost over, and we will not be gone from Viosk for long.'

'How long is eternity?' the *badchan* muttered.

Hannah tried to speak again, but this time Gitl's hand covered her entire mouth. 'Be still, child,' Gitl whispered. 'Whatever your objections, be still. This is not one of your stories that ends happy-ever-after. There are not imaginary bullets in those guns. Listen to the rabbi. He is right to calm us. If we go quietly, no harm will come.'

Suddenly remembering the pictures on television, the ones that made her grandfather so crazy, Hannah shook her head. But she shook it silently, as Gitl commanded. She wanted to cry. She knew she'd feel better if she could. But no tears came. Drawing a deep breath, she heard the rabbi begin to pray aloud.

'*Shema Yisrael, Adonai eloheynu, Adonai echod.* Hear, O Israel the Lord our God, the Lord is One.'

The others joined in. Even Hannah.

They climbed into the trucks in family groups, reluctant to be parted. Since Shmuel would not let go of Fayge's hand despite the rabbi's fierce stare, the rabbi was forced to climb into the truck with them, standing next to Hannah.

Yitzchak handed his children up to Gitl one at a time, and she kept her arms tight around the little girl, Tzipporah. There were finally so many villagers packed into each truck, there was no room to sit down. So they stood, the children up on the men's shoulders. They looked like holidayers off on a trip. But they felt to Hannah, all crushed together, like cattle going to be slaughtered for the market.

The trucks barreled down the long, winding road, their passengers silenced by the dust deviling up and by the heat. After a bit, to keep the children in her truck from crying, Gitl began to sing. First she tried a lullaby called 'Yankele' to quiet them, then several children's songs. But as the truck continued without a stop, carrying them farther and farther from Viosk, onto roads most of them had never seen, she broke into a song that, for all its wailing minor notes and the *lalala* chorus, sounded angry.

Hannah tried to make out the words above the noise of the truck. They were about someone called a *chaper*, a snatcher or kidnapper, who dragged men off to the army. One verse went:

Sir, give me a piece of bread,
Look at me, so pale and dead.

It hardly seemed a song to calm the children. But first Shmuel, then Yitzchak, then several of the other men in their truck joined in, singing at the top of their voices. The children on their perches clapped in rhythm. At last, even Fayge and her father began to sing.

Hannah listened to the growing chorus in wonder, as the song leaped from truck to truck down the long road. Didn't they know? Didn't they guess? Didn't they care? She kept remembering more and more, bits and pieces of her classroom discussions about the Holocaust. About the death camps and the crematoria. About the brutal Nazis and the six million dead Jews. Was knowing – or not knowing – more frightening? She couldn't decide. A strange awful taste rose in her mouth, more bitter even than the Seder's bitter herbs. And *they* were for remembering. She fought the taste down. She would not, she *could* not be sick. Not here. Not now. She opened her mouth to catch a breath of air, and found herself singing. The sound of her own voice drowned out the steady drone of the tires on the endless, twisting road.

10

'LOOK!' SHMUEL cried over the noise of the singing.

At his voice, everyone suddenly quieted, following his pointing hand. Ahead of them was a train station, its windows sparkling in the bright spring sun. There were armed guards standing in front of the station house door and scattered around the periphery. Two wooden boxcars squatted on a nearby siding.

The trucks pulled up to the station house. Jumping out of the cabs, the soldiers called up to the villagers, 'Get out. Out. Quickly.'

When no one moved, the soldiers raised their guns.

Shmuel put his hands on the raised panel, and leaped down. Yitzchak handed his son down to Shmuel, then jumped down himself. The other men climbed out, turned, lifted their arms to take the children. Then the women and girls, clumsier in their party skirts, climbed down with help from the men. Fayge's wedding dress caught on a protruding nail. When she had to rip it loose, she began to cry and could not be comforted.

'Quickly, quickly,' the soldiers called, gesturing with their guns. Rounding up the villagers, they herded them toward the trains.

There were piles of things spread out along the tracks, as if they had been dropped by a fleeing army. Hannah saw suitcases and carpetbags, some carefully packed and some with their contents spilling out. Dresses and shawls were scattered around, and there was a bag of what looked like medicines, several dozen jewelry cases, a sackful of milk powder, even a small chest of baby toys.

'That is Grandma's satchel,' Fayge shrieked, pointing to a tapestry bag with wooden handles. 'Papa, Papa, they have left Grandma's things here. What will she use in the resettlement camp?'

Before the rabbi could answer, Hannah had turned to Gitl. 'I know . . .'

'Do not say a word, child,' Gitl pleaded. 'Not a word.'

More and more, the villagers began to recognize baskets and bags belonging to their families. But they were not allowed to stop by the piles, simply pushed closer to the boxcars. When the last of them was out of the trucks, the soldiers made a great circle around them. A high-ranking officer – but not the colonel who had spoken to them before – stepped into the circle with them. They looked to him and he raised his hand for silence.

'Now, Jews, listen. Do what you are told and no one will be hurt. All I ask is your cooperation.' His voice was ragged, as if it had been used too much recently. He had a dark blond mustache and bad teeth.

Hannah felt Gitl's arm tighten on her shoulder, and

the villagers began to murmur among themselves. Hannah held her breath. If she held it for long enough, she thought she might wake up from this awful nightmare and be back safe at her family Seder. But when she had to let her breath out at last, she began to cough desperately and Gitl pounded her on the back.

'. . . lie down' was all she heard.

'What? Here? On the ground?' someone cried out.

'Of course, Jew,' came the officer's voice. 'And then my men will move among you and take your papers and jewelry for safekeeping.'

'You mean for your *own* keeping,' a man called out. Hannah thought it might have been Shmuel.

'Who said that?' the officer asked. When no one answered, he narrowed his eyes. 'The next one who speaks I will shoot.'

There was silence so profound, Hannah wondered if she had gone deaf.

'Now – lie down!' the officer commanded at last. He gestured with his hand and the soldiers behind him made the same movement with their guns. When still no one moved, the officer very slowly and deliberately removed the pistol from his holster and pointed it at the feet of a man standing near the edge of the crowd. He fired a single shot. Dirt and pebbles sprayed up and several women screamed. A little girl cried out, 'Mama, Mama, Mama.' Hannah was suddenly so cold she couldn't move.

Gitl shoved her in the back. 'Lie down,' she whispered. 'Lie down, quickly.'

Hannah fell to the ground on her stomach and

didn't stir. When she finally forced herself to open her eyes, there was a pair of large boots by her head. She could hear children whimpering and somewhere, off to her left, a woman was crying. There was a low undercurrent of men's voices. It took a moment before she realized they were praying.

Hours later – or so it seemed – they were allowed to stand up again. Gitl had her hand up to her neck. There was a red mark that ran around it as if a necklace had been torn from her. Fayge's beaded headdress and her earrings were gone. Her dress was smudged and torn. Several men were bleeding from their noses and Shmuel had a dark bruise starting at his temple. But except for the quiet snuffling of the children, a man's persistent hacking cough, and Rachel's labored breathing, no one made a sound.

'Now,' the officer said, smiling down at them and showing his rotten teeth, 'now, Jews, you are ready for resettlement.'

'Where?' a tremulous voice called out.

'Wherever we choose to send you,' he answered. 'Get up.'

They stood raggedly, and the soldiers herded them toward the two stationary boxcars. They went silently, almost willingly, eager to be as far from the officer and the soldiers' guns as they could.

'But, Gitl,' Hannah whispered her protest as she stared at the two cars, 'we can't all fit in there.'

'With God's help . . . ,' Gitl mumbled, squeezing Hannah's hand until her knuckles hurt.

The older people were pushed into the boxcars first, then the women and the girls. Someone shoved Hannah from behind so hard, she scraped her knee climbing up. She could feel the blood flowing down and the sharp gritty pain, but before she could bend over to look at it, someone else was behind her. Soon there were so many people crowded in, she couldn't move at all. It was worse than the worst subway jam she'd ever been in, shopping with her Aunt Eva in the city. She was caught between Gitl on one side and the rabbi on the other. There were two women behind her and the boards of the boxcar by her face. By bending her good knee just a little, she could see out a small rectangular space between the boards. She'd just gotten a look when the car shifted and the door was shut and bolted from the outside.

'We're locked in!' a woman screamed. 'My God, we'll suffocate.'

Everyone began to scream then, Hannah with them. The ones by the door hammered on it with their fists, the car rocking with their efforts, but it did no good. No one came to open the door. After a while, exhausted by all the screaming and the tears, they stopped.

It was pretty dark inside the car, with only small patches of light where the boards did not quite fit together. And it was airless. And hot. One of the two women directly behind Hannah smelled of garlic. Somewhere a child cried out that she had to go to the bathroom. A little while later, a smell announced that she had.

'How long?' someone called out.

The rabbi's voice replied calmly, 'We are in God's hands now.'

'God's hands are very hot and sweaty,' Gitl said.

'How can you say such a thing?' It was Fayge.

Just then the car shook and everybody screamed.

'I hear a train,' Hannah cried out. She bent her good knee again and looked through the crack. A dark engine was coming down the track, backing toward them. 'I see it.'

'God's hands, my children,' the rabbi said loudly.

As the engine bumped against the two cars, shaking them and making it hard to stand, Hannah managed to twist just enough to speak directly to the rabbi. 'Please, Rabbi,' she pleaded, 'we must *do* something. And quickly. I know where they're taking us. I am . . . I am . . . from the future. *Please.*'

Rabbi Boruch cleared his voice before speaking. 'All children are from the future. I am from the past. And the past tells us what we must do in the future. That is why adults do the teaching and children the learning. So you must listen to me when I tell you that what we must do now is pray. Pray, for we are all in God's hands.

Gitl was right, Hannah thought. God's hands were very hot and sweaty. The stench in the crowded boxcar was overwhelming, a powerful stew of human perspiration and fear and the smell of children being sick. As the train clacketed along the tracks, Hannah thought how lucky she was to be near a pocket of fresh air. Most of the others were not so fortunate.

For the longest time, no one spoke. But after an hour, the silence was too depressing and voices volunteered what comfort they could.

'I can see a little bit,' a man near the door said. 'We are passing a town. Now I see peasants in the field.'

Spontaneously several voices cried out, 'Help! Help us!'

'Any reaction?' Yitzchak asked.

'Yes. They ran their fingers across their throats.'

'The bastards. Do they care nothing?' a woman asked.

Shmuel answered, 'Did they ever?'

A man with a deep, rough voice spoke. 'I hear there was another shtetl taken to a railroad station somewhere in Russia.'

'Why resettle Russian Jews? Russia is not big enough for all?'

'Big enough so a story could get lost there. So tell us, *where* in Russia?' Gitl said.

'Who knows where?' the man called out. 'What does the *where* matter? The shtetl is no longer there anyway. But wherever it was, the villagers were made to lie down in trenches, like herring, head to foot. And then, Lord God, they were slaughtered as they lay there, by soldiers with machine guns. Lime was put on top of them when they were still warm and the next ones were made to lie down on top of that. Six times they made herrings. Six times. Until they were all dead.'

A woman, her voice edged with hysteria, said, 'You heard, you heard, but if they were all dead, how could anyone know for sure?'

The man coughed, and continued without answering her, 'When they made us lie down, I remembered what I had heard.'

Another woman said, 'But they did not kill us. Just made us a *bissel* uncomfortable.'

'Uncomfortable! They took my wedding ring. They kicked my Avrom in the nose. Uncomfortable!' It was a third woman.

'It is just a story' the first woman said. 'A nightmare. Do not tell us any more of your awful stories.'

The man coughed again, then said, 'Is it not written that we must bear witness?'

'What witness?' Fayge cried. 'Were you there? It is only gossip. Vicious, cruel gossip. Rumors. Shmuel, tell him it is only that.'

Shmuel was silent.

'Not gossip, Fayge. It's true. I know . . . ,' Hannah said.

Gitl pinched her above the shoulder to silence her.

The man spoke again. 'The one who told me was a distant cousin. He knew someone who escaped.'

'You said no one escaped' Fayge put in.

'Hush,' a woman near Hannah said. 'The children will hear you and be afraid.'

'I heard . . . ,' another man began. Hannah recognized Yitzchak's voice. 'I heard another story when I was in Liansk buying poultry. There was a doctor, a fine man, very educated. He was operating in the hospital on a Christian woman. She trusted him more than her own, you see. And right in the middle of the operation, because her husband had called them in, the soldiers came and dragged the doctor away and killed him. With his own instruments. In front of his family.'

'Did the woman die? The shikse he was operating on?' another man asked.

'I hope so,' a light voice chorused.

'No,' Yitzchak said. 'She did not die. And she did not deserve to die.'

'Perhaps *she* did not,' Gitl said. 'But her husband did. And the soldiers. Monsters.'

'Hush,' the woman near Hannah said again. 'The children will hear you.'

The rabbi cleared his throat loudly. 'These are just rumors and gossip. The proverbs say 'He who harps on a matter alienates his friend.'

'Well, I heard' – a man's voice came from the back of the car. He spoke so softly at first that the people near him shushed the others so he might be heard. 'I heard, and reliably, too, that in a town on the border of Poland, the entire population was locked *in* the synagogue. And then the Nazis set fire to the building. Anyone trying to jump out the windows was shot. Only there was a Pole, a good man, the *Shabbos goy*, who opened the back door, so a few of the villagers escaped and were hidden by the *Shabbos goy* in his own house. In his own house! I had a friend who was one of the seven who got out. He told me the smell of people burning is not unlike the smell of cooking pigs.'

'Hah!' said Gitl. 'And how does he – a good Jew

know what pigs smell like cooking?'

'So – so he was not kosher. Or the *Shabbos goy* told him.'

'So!'

'How can you joke about such things?' Hannah said in a very small voice.

Gitl made a *tching* sound with her tongue. 'If we do not laugh, we will cry. Crying will only make us hotter and sweatier. We Jews like to joke about death because what you laugh at and make familiar can no longer frighten you. Besides, Chayaleh, what else is there to do?'

'Hush,' the woman near Hannah remarked again, 'the children.'

'We could break down the doors and run away,' Hannah said.

'Run away? Where, little Chaya? To Lublin?' Gitl asked.

'To America,' Hannah said.

'To be with Avrom Morowitz? *This* is my home.'

'This boxcar?' Hannah whispered.

'Do not be impudent.'

'To Israel then.'

Gitl laughed, a strange, hollow sound. 'And where is Israel,' she asked, 'except in our prayers?'

'Hush,' the woman begged.

The stories continued.

'Did you hear about Mostochowa?' a man asked.

'You mean the place where they were all forced out of their houses to stand naked in the snow?' Yitzchak said.

'Rumors,' the rabbi cautioned.

'They were beaten,' a woman said.

'Yes, Masha is right, beaten unmercifully. And the blood on the snow, my Uncle Moishe who was there said, was like rose petals falling. Rose petals, he said,' the man concluded.

'No more stories!' Fayge shouted. 'Nothing more will happen to us. Nothing. We are uncomfortable and crowded. We are hungry. But it will pass. We are going to be resettled. That is all. And then I will be married. *With* a canopy.'

'I heard . . .'

'Hush! Hush!' The woman near Hannah spoke in tired spurts of sound. 'The children can stand no more. My child is senseless with all this talk.'

A voice close to her said quietly, 'Let me take the child, mother. I will hold her for a while.' There was a small movement as everyone tried to adjust. 'Oh, my God, the child is not senseless. The child is dead. *Boruch dayan emes*. Blessed be the righteous judge . . .'

Hannah wept.

11

THE BOXCARS TRAVELED for four days and nights; the only difference that Hannah could tell was in the heat. Under the midday sun, it was like standing in an oven, an oven that smelled of human sweat and urine and feces. But at night, when it was cold, they were all grateful for the close quarters.

The train made only two stops the entire time. At Troniat, a small station that one of the men recognized, the doors were suddenly thrown open and they tumbled out into the darkness onto a gravel path.

That was when they discovered that three old women had died and a fourth was near death and could not climb out of the car. All four of the bodies were slung out by the soldiers onto a siding. The dead baby was torn from its mother's arms and cast behind a horse's watering trough. The child's mother began to wail, but her husband slapped his hand across her mouth, whispering, 'Hush, hush, hush.'

A bucket of filthy trough water was passed around, and everyone grabbed for it eagerly. Hannah managed a mouthful before it was taken from her. There was hay in that mouthful, but she didn't care. She'd never tasted anything so sweet.

A feeble pounding came from the other boxcar.

'For God's sake,' Shmuel cried out, 'open the doors for them.' But the soldiers ignored him, hurrying the bucket along.

At the second stop, they heard the grateful cries of their neighbors as they were led from the other boxcar. But pound as they might on the slats, their own door remained shut.

'Monsters!' Gitl said, her voice a croak. 'Monsters!'

It was the last thing any of them said on the moving train.

On the fourth day, the train slowed, the noise of its wheels a terrifying shriek. Hannah felt hope, like a small bubble, rise from her empty stomach. Her mouth was so dry, she could feel her tongue as big as a sausage between her teeth. Letting out a deep, sighing breath, she heard echoes of that sigh all around her.

The train jerked to a stop and the silence was like a prayer. Into that silence, the raw scraping of the doors being pulled open was as loud as thunder. Air, fresh air, rushed in. Hannah tried to suck in as much as she could.

''Raus, 'raus, schneller!' came the harsh command. 'Out, out, faster!'

They scrambled out of the boxcar to stand, blinking in the early morning light. Hannah's knees trembled from the effort of moving, and her head felt light from all the fresh air. When she looked around, she could see how weakened everyone was. Only Gitl, her dark green dress crumpled, the white collar torn, held her head high. She had an arm under Fayge's, steadying her. Fayge's white wedding dress was badly stained, front and back, and she was as pale as paper. Yitzchak, carrying both his daughter and his son in his arms, was still gulping at the air. The children did not move. And Shmuel – Hannah could not find him. Then she saw he was still standing in the door of the boxcar.

'There are more dead here,' he called.

'Leave them!' a soldier said, slamming his rifle butt into Shmuel's shins. 'Get down.'

Shmuel got down painfully, and hobbled over to Gitl's side. He put his hand on Hannah's hair tenderly, but it felt as heavy as a weight.

'There are five old women from Viosk, and old Shimshon the tailor in there,' he whispered. Then under his breath he muttered, 'And a child.'

'*Boruch dayan emes . . . ,*' Gitl said.

'Down there!' a soldier shouted, gesturing with his rifle. Part of the moon still hung in the sky, a pale halo over his blond head.

Hannah followed the line of his pointing gun. Below them, down a gravel embankment, was a stark line of low barracks. She tried to count them; they seemed to go on and on. A barbed wire fence surrounded them. To the side of the barracks was a small, pretty house where early spring flowers were opening. A wrought-iron gate stood in front of the buildings, and over the gate was a sign proclaiming in large black letters: ARBEIT MACHT FREI.

Several of the villagers whispered the words, but the rabbi, his hand up to his eyes, strained to read them.

'What does it say, Faygeleh?' he asked, clinging to his daughter's hand, suddenly an old man. 'My eyes...'

But Fayge was beyond answering. It was Hannah who told him, her voice bitter. 'Work makes you free,' she said.

The rabbi nodded. 'See, my children,' he said hoarsely, 'we are in God's hands. We are not afraid of work.'

Behind him, the *badchan* whispered, 'This is the Devil's work, not God's.'

'Down there,' the blond soldier called out again. '*Schnell!*'

They were forced by the soldiers to scramble down the high gravel embankment, and the slippery stones slid away underfoot. Hannah went down on her bad knee and cried out once. Behind her, Fayge tried to sidestep so as not to bump into her, stumbled, fell, and began to roll faster and faster downhill until she hit the bottom with a horrible thudding sound. Her white skirts were rucked up over her thighs. Shmuel ran after her, knelt by her side, and cradled her in his arms. Smoothing her skirts down, he whispered, 'My bride, my bride.' Fayge didn't move.

'Get up! Get up! Men to the left, women to the right!' All the soldiers were shouting now. One pushed Shmuel to his feet. The children were torn from Yitzchak's arms and shoved toward the women's group. Little Reuven began to whimper, but the girl,

Tzipporah, was silent.

It was Gitl who pulled Fayge up. Fayge looked dazed. Tears ran down her dirty cheeks, leaving gray runnels. Hurrying over, Hannah offered to help.

'What can I do?' she asked.

'What can any of us do?' Fayge murmured.

'See, I was right,' Hannah whispered to Gitl. 'Why didn't you believe me? I was right all along. We should have run.'

'Run,' Fayge said, catching the last word, and repeated it in a soft, uninflected voice. 'Run.'

Gitl shook her head. 'There is nowhere to run, Fayge. We are where we are. Hush.' Then she turned her head and stared at the soldiers. 'Monsters,' she said, loud enough for them to hear.

'You are *zugangi*, newcomers, the lowest of the low,' the tall, dark-haired woman said to them as they huddled in the stark barracks room. She was in a blue dress with green piping and the short sleeves displayed a long number tattooed on her arm.

"But, that number . . . then you are a prisoner, too,' Hannah blurted out. She'd been thinking that they would have to wear striped pajamas like the prisoners in the old photographs, yet she'd seen no one dressed like that in the camp yet. Maybe that meant her memories were false ones. Maybe things wouldn't be as bad as she feared.

'I am a prisoner – yes,' the woman said. 'But I am not a Jew. See . . .' She held up her arm so that the blue number was plain.

Whatever it was they were supposed to read there baffled the women and they murmured together.

'Quiet. You do not speak unless spoken to. I am a prisoner, but you are *zugangi*, newcomers. And one of the first lessons you have to learn is not to call attention to yourselves. You, girl, who spoke out, you will give me those blue ribbons in your hair.'

'No!' said Hannah, surprised at the vehemence in her response. 'They aren't mine to give. You can't have them.'

The woman came over to her and slapped her hard on both cheeks. 'You never say no here. Not if you want to live. I will have those ribbons. They go with my dress.'

Hand on her burning right cheek, Hannah drew in a deep breath, willing herself not to cry.

Gitl poked Hannah in the side and whispered, 'Give them to her. What do two little ribbons matter?' Swiftly she began to unbraid Hannah's left braid. Reluctantly, Hannah undid the right.

'Good,' the woman said, stuffing the ribbons into a pocket in her dress. 'And now you will all go in there.' She pointed down a narrow hall. '*Schnell*. It is a most important word that you should learn. Whether I say it or the Germans say it, it is to be obeyed. *Schnell!*'

They hurried through the hall and found themselves in a kind of amphitheater. Hannah noticed Shifre and Yente standing together, holding hands. Esther was next to a tall, scowling woman, probably her mother.

The woman in the blue dress was speaking again.

'Quiet! Quiet!' she shouted, putting up her hands. 'Now, since you are all filthy from your trip, you must take a shower. You will undress here. Help the children. It must be done quickly. Quickly.'

'What, here?' Gitl asked. 'In front of each other?'

The woman looked disgusted. 'You have not learned the first lesson yet. You will not last here.'

Gitl stared at her. 'I will last,' she said, her voice low.

'Now, all of you, undress. *Schnell!* Pretend you are in one of your ritual baths. Oh yes, I am not a Jew, but even I have heard of it. What do you call it?'

'*Mikvah,*' murmured Esther's mother.

'Yes, *mikvah,*' the woman said. 'Then this is your *mikvah* in preparation for your new life in the camp.' She smiled and left.

Some of the women sat on the wooden benches and began slowly to take off their shoes and stockings. But Hannah stood in the center of the room, staring around.

'Don't you understand?' she cried. 'There are no showers. There are only the gas ovens. They will burn us all up.'

Two benches away, Esther was crying softly as she took off her right shoe. 'There are no ovens, Chaya. Do not try to frighten us. We are frightened enough.'

Hannah started to answer but Giti pulled her down to the bench. 'She is right, child. What is here is bad enough. Let us live moment by moment. There is no harm in dreaming about a shower. God knows we could all use one.'

Hannah was furious. They *had* to listen. She would have to make them. What use was her special fore-knowledge if no one would listen? Maybe they thought her strange or sick or even crazy, but she was none of that. She was from the future, somehow. She could summon up those memories by trying really hard. She knew she could help them all if only they would let her. Then she looked up. The women and the other girls were shyly, painfully, slowly taking off their clothes. Hannah thought they looked so vulner-able, so helpless. Yet they had a kind of innocence about them and a kind of hope. All they were looking forward to was the shower. Biting her lower lip, she thought what her knowledge of the ovens, of the bru-tal guards, of names like Auschwitz and Dachau could really do for them here, naked and weaponless, except to take away that moment by moment of hope. Maybe Gitl was right. *We are where we are.* She would not add more to their misery. She bent over and untied her shoes.

They waited nearly twenty minutes in the cold room and the silence was frightening. Beside Hannah, Gitl began to sing a quiet song about dreaming. 'Dreaming is better, dreaming is brighter,' she sang. Esther, Yente, and Shifre joined in.

Hannah looked around the room, then leaned over and whispered to Esther. 'Where is Rachel?'

Esther kept on singing, but tears ran down her cheeks. 'Dreaming is brighter.'

'Where is she?' Hannah insisted, though her question seemed to lack authority, with both of them sitting naked, goosebumps scattered over their arms and thighs.

Esther stopped singing all at once and looked down at her bare legs. At last she spoke. 'Rachel always had trouble breathing in the spring.'

Hannah remembered the peculiar breathy hesitations Rachel had made when she spoke.

'Did she have . . . trouble breathing . . . in the boxcar?' Hannah asked. She began to shake even before Esther's answer, though she wasn't sure why. 'Is she . . . is she . . . dead?'

'Dreams are better,' Esther sang, her voice breaking on a high note.

Hannah opened her mouth and found herself sucking in air in great gulps. She couldn't stop. After about seven big breaths, she said, to no one in particular, 'I should have told her she was my best friend. I should have said yes. I . . .'

Suddenly the doors were flung open and two soldiers marched in, their boots loud on the wooden floor.

'*Achtung!*' one shouted, a young man with a wandering left eye.

The girls screamed, turning their backs, and the younger women tried to cover themselves with their hands. Fayge bent over at the waist and her long black hair was like a blanket over her. The older women didn't move.

'Into the showers,' the soldier with the bad eye called. 'And then you visit the barber.'

Hannah stood slowly, thinking: *I will be brave. I am the only one who knows about the ovens, but I will be brave. I will not take away their hope, which is all they have. I will not tell them that the Nazis often lied and said people were going to take showers when they took them to be killed.* Her legs were weak. She felt she could not make one foot go in front of the other. She was glad that Gitl's hand was at her elbow the entire time.

The showers were ice cold, but Hannah was so relieved it was water – and not the gas she'd expected – that she stood under the sprinklers a long time. She tilted her head back and opened her mouth, drinking in the cold drops until her belly was full.

Suddenly the showers were turned off.

'*Schnell, schnell!*' the soldiers shouted, ushering them back, without towels, into the cold room.

Head down, hands over her breasts, Hannah walked through the line of soldiers, remembering how childish she'd thought the blue dress and longing for it.

Their clothes were gone. With nothing to dry themselves and no clothes to put on, they waited, shivering, in the bare room. The children began to make small, whimpering sounds and Hannah had to stop herself from joining in.

Just then the door from the outside opened and a soldier escorted a short, dark man into the room.

'Here is the barber,' the soldier said. 'You will make a line for him and he will do his job. There will be no noise. Remember – no hair, no lice.'

Lice? Hannah thought. *We have no lice.*

The barber was clearly a prisoner. His own head was shaved, and with the bones so prominent on his face, he looked to be all forehead and nose. He cut their hair without any discernible skill, often pulling great clumps out with the blunt scissors. Shifre's two pale braids came off whole, landing with a soft *thud-thud* on the floor. She touched one with a bare foot, as if the plait were some sort of unknown animal. Fayge's curls, tight from the shower, scattered across the floor like patterns in a rug. Little Tzipporah screamed in terror at her turn until a woman held her tightly.

When the man came to Hannah, she bit her lip so as not to cry and kept her eyes closed the entire time. She concentrated on what was to happen next – after the showers and the hair-cutting, remembering from the lessons in Holocaust history in school. But as the scissors *snip-snapped* through her hair and the razor shaved the rest, she realized with a sudden awful panic that she could no longer recall anything from the past. *I cannot remember*, she whispered to herself. *I cannot remember.* She'd been shorn of memory as brutally as she'd been shorn of her hair, without permission, without reason. Opening her eyes, she stared at the floor. Clots of wet hair lay all about: dark hair, light hair, short hair, long hair, and two pale braids. *Gone, all gone,* she thought again wildly, no longer even sure what was gone, what she was mourning.

She looked up and couldn't recognize anyone in the room. Without their hair, all the women looked the same.

'Gitl,' she cried out, speaking the one name she recalled. 'Gitl, where are you?' Her voice cracked and, without meaning to, she began to sob almost soundlessly.

Someone's arms went around her and the touch of skin on skin made her shiver. Everything felt strange, alien, as if she were on another planet, as if she were on the moon.

'Gitl?' she whispered to the stranger with the shaved head who was holding her.

'Yes, child,' Gitl answered. 'But promise me you will cry no more before these monsters. We will never cry again.'

'Never' Hannah agreed, wiping her eyes with the back of her hand and feeling stronger because of the promise. 'Never.'

12

THEY SAT ON THE BENCHES naked and cold for a long time while the barber worked on each in turn. Hannah glanced around cautiously. With their hair gone, they all looked like little old men. She wondered what she looked like herself, resisting the urge to put her hand up to her head again. She would not think about it. Thinking was dangerous. In this place she would not think, only do.

After a while, time seemed to lose its reality. Only the *snick-snack* of the scissors and the occasional cry of the barber's victims marked the minutes. There was a dreamlike feeling in the room as if, Hannah thought, anything might happen next.

The woman in the blue dress entered the far door and stood for a long moment examining them all with a sour face. Hannah happened to be facing the door when she entered and, without meaning to, locked eyes with her. It was the woman who looked away first, calling out, '*Schnell!* Into the next room. You must have clothes.' She turned abruptly, signaling with her hand. For the first time Hannah noticed that she had only three fingers on her right hand.

I wonder how she lost those fingers, Hannah thought. *Was she born that way?* Then remembered she was not going to think. She rose with the others and shuffled out of the room after them.

For the first time, Hannah allowed herself to feel hungry. But when she began to wonder about when they might be fed, the still, small voice reminded her, *Don't think, do.* She reached out and found the hand of one of the children. Silently she squeezed the child's hand for comfort.

The room they were herded into was a small, low-ceilinged place with a single window high up under the eaves. It reminded Hannah of an attic somewhere, she couldn't remember where. An unadorned light bulb dangled down over several long wooden tables piled high with rags.

'*Shmattes!*' whispered a woman behind Hannah in a hoarse voice.

'Choose!' bellowed the three-fingered woman in blue. '*Schnell!*'

Hannah took her turn at one of the tables and started to paw through the clothes. They were ragged and worn and smelled peculiar, with a lingering, dank odor, part old sweat and part something else Hannah did not even want to guess at. She hesitated.

'Choose, Jews. You cannot be fancy now.'

Don't think. Do. Hannah put her hand onto the pile and came up with a dark gray dress with a dirty white collar and cuffs. There was a ragged rip along the hem and deep perspiration stains under the arms. Looking around, she saw that the other women were already

95

slipping into whatever they had chosen. She raised the gray dress over her head and pulled it down. The material was silky and a bit stiff where it was stained. Buttoning the three buttons in front, she remembered suddenly how she had thought the dark blue dress Gitl had given her ugly, how she'd called it a rag. Even that small return of memory was a comfort. She'd called the dress a rag; she hadn't known anything about wearing rags then. Her arms strained the sleeves of the gray dress.

'Help the children,' someone near her whispered. It sounded like Gitl.

Hannah glanced down at the naked child by her side. Was it Tzipporah? The poor little thing had her thumb in her mouth. Her eyelids were a bruised bluish color and she swayed where she stood. Hannah rummaged quickly through the pile of clothes and found a blouse and jumper that looked as if they might fit. The child made no move to help, and Hannah had to dress her as if she were a doll, pushing her arms into the sleeves of the blouse as gently as she could.

They were herded directly into another room and made to line up single file. Another shaven-headed prisoner, with an odd-looking metal instrument, sat at a wooden table. There were guards at the door.

Hannah could hear a mumble of voices by the table, but she couldn't begin to guess what they were discussing. Holding Tzipporah's hand, she moved in the slow, shuffling barefooted rhythm of the line: wait, walk, wait, walk.

Closer to the table, she saw that the man was using the instrument to write something on each woman's arm. Strangely, no one protested or drew their arm away.

Another memory, hazier than the one about the dress, flooded back to her. *'This . . .'* She heard a familiar man's voice crying out. *'I'll give them this!'* She couldn't think who it was or what he was giving to whom. When she turned to see who was speaking, everyone behind her was silent, staring at the floor.

'Next!'

The man meant Hannah. She walked up to the table and sat down on a chair by the side of the table.

'Tell me your name,' the man said. 'I will give you a number in exchange.'

That seemed simple enough, but she couldn't think of a name. There was none that came to her. From behind, Gitl whispered hoarsely, 'Chaya. Chaya Abramowicz.'

She said it aloud. 'Chaya.' It felt – and it did not feel – like hers.

The man looked at her and his eyes were the saddest she'd ever seen, a muddy brown, like river sludge. His mouth was puckered and old. It dropped open as easily as a slot in a machine, and a sound – not quite a cry – came out.

'I knew it would come' he whispered. 'Some day. The *malach ha-mavis.'*

'What? What?' Hannah asked.

'That is my daughter's dress you are wearing, Chaya Abramowicz. My Chaya. I brought it as a present for her in Lublin.'

'Chaya,' Hannah said.

'The same name, too. God is good. Your name means life.' His voice broke.

'Life,' Hannah repeated.

He nodded, then shook his head, the one following the other like a single movement. 'You are Chaya no longer, child. Now you are J197241. Remember it.'

'I can't remember anything,' Hannah said, puzzled.

'This you must remember, for if you forget it, *life* is gone indeed.' The tattooing pen burned her flesh, leaving a trail of blue numbers in her arm above the wrist. J197241. She didn't cry. She wouldn't. It was something more she just remembered: her promise to Gitl.

When the man finished the number, he reached out and touched the collar of her dress, smoothing it down gently. 'Live,' he whispered. 'For my Chaya. For all our Chayas. Live. And remember.'

There was a loud clearing of a throat and Hannah looked up into the guard's unsmiling face. 'Next!' he said.

Little Tzipporah was next, and Hannah held the child on her lap, covering her eyes with ice-cold hands and crooning a song into her ears. It was a wedding song, the only song she could come up with, something about a madness forced upon them. The words didn't matter, only the melody, only the soothing rhythm. The child, Tzipporah, J197242, lay silent in her arms.

The barracks they were assigned had a long brick oven

along one end and deep trenches on the sides in which sleeping shelves were placed, like triple bunk beds, at impossibly narrow intervals. Privies were outside.

Hannah helped Tzipporah onto one of the low shelves. There were neither blankets nor pillows, but the child did not complain. She curled into a fetal position and lay still, her thumb back in her mouth.

'I will see if there is any food,' Hannah whispered to her. 'And socks. And shoes. I will see if there are blankets. Or pillows. You sleep.' When she stood up, she saw Gitl helping Fayge onto another shelf, about halfway down the building. She knew it was Fayge because, even with her hair shorn, her face the color of an old book, and wearing a shapeless brown print dress, Fayge had an unearthly beauty. But her eyes were strangely blank; she moved where Gitl pushed her.

Gitl looked up and stared at Hannah. Putting her hands on her hips, barely covering the garish flowers on the red print dress, she smiled mockingly. 'So?'

'So!' Hannah whispered back. In that dark, cold place it seemed a kind of affirmation. At that very moment, her stomach rumbled, horribly loud in the silence of the barracks room. That, too, had the sound of life.

Gitl's head went back and she roared with laughter.

'How can you laugh?' Hannah asked, shocked.

'How can you not?' Gitl said. 'Without laughter, there is no hope. Without hope, there is no life. Without life . . .'

'Without life . . .' Hannah's voice trailed off, remembering the old tattooer.

'Without *food* there is no life,' Gitl said. 'We will go and see if any of these monsters believes in food.'

The moment they tried to set a foot outside, a guard blocked their way. With their Yiddish, they were just able to understand his German.

'You will not leave,' he said, his baby face stern.

'We have children in here who have not eaten for days,' Gitl answered.

'They will get used to it,' the soldier said as if the words were rote in his mouth. 'They will get used to it.'

'Just like the farmer who trained his horse to eat less and less,' said Gitl. 'And just when he had gotten it to the point of learning to eat nothing at all, the ingrate up and died. I suppose you have heard that story?'

'I hear nothing important from Jews,' the soldier said. 'But I have something important to tell them. See that?' He pointed to a brick chimney towering over a flat-roofed building where a thin line of smoke curled lazily into the air. 'That's Jew smoke! Learn to eat when it's given to you, Jew, or you, too, go up that stack.'

'Jew smoke?' Gitl whispered. But the soldier was already closing the door against her protesting hands.

Hannah bit her lip. The smokestack and the ominous black curl emerging from it, dissipating against the bright blue sky, reminded her of something. Yet she couldn't quite touch it. It slipped away from her. Something about smoke. About fire. About ovens.

'Oven,' she whispered.

'Well,' Gitl said, 'at least we know something.'

Hannah looked up at her, the slip of memory gone. 'What?'

'That we *will* be fed.'

'When?'

'God only knows. And let us hope that He tells the Germans!'

They turned back to stare around them, straining into the darkness of the barracks. Hannah saw that almost all the sleeping shelves were filled. The women and children lay as still as corpses.

'Look, not even the thought of food tempts them,' Gitl said.

Hannah could not keep herself from rubbing her eyes. The thought of sleep, horizontal sleep, suddenly overwhelmed her.

'What am I thinking of?' Gitl said, the heel of her palm striking her forehead. 'You are only a child. You need sleep as well as food.' She put her hand out to touch Hannah on the head and then, as if thinking better of it, patted her instead on the shoulder. 'Go to sleep, Chaya.'

'Go to sleep . . .' Hannah glanced down at her wrist. 'Go to sleep, J197241, you mean.'

'You are a name, not a number. Never forget that name, whatever they tell you here. You will always be Chaya – *life* – to me. You are my brother's child. You are my blood.'

Hannah shook her head slowly, but neither she nor Gitl knew what she really meant by it. She rubbed her fingers across the numbers on her sore arm as if memorizing them. Then she let Gitl lead her to an unoccupied shelf, where she rolled herself onto it and, without even minding the rough surface, fell asleep.

She dreamed of roast beef, sweet wine, and bitter herbs.

13

HANNAH WOKE TO A strange mechanical bellowing. For a moment, she thought it was the clock radio
by her bed. She sat up suddenly and hit her head with
a loud crack on the shelf above her. Stunned, she
looked around. *Clock radio*? The words sat lumpily in
her mind. She was not sure what a *clock radio* was.
Besides, her head hurt where she'd banged it and her
back ached from lying on the hard shelf. Even her leg
hurt. She drew her knee up to look. There was caked
blood and a big scab along her shin.

Then she remembered: the trip in the cattle car, the
long hungry days, the heat and the cold, the smell, the
dead baby, the tattoo, the shorn hair. Cautiously she
reached up and felt her head. What hair was left was a
stubble. She did not dare look at the number on her
arm.

Swinging her legs carefully over the side of the
shelf, she eased herself onto the floor, aware that the
bellowing horn had stopped. Others in the barracks
were performing the same slow unfolding. She looked
around, her eyes and mind still fuzzed with sleep.

The door to the barracks was flung open and a guard

stuck his head in.

'If you want food, get in line. Now. *Schnell*. You must eat. Hungry Jews are dead Jews. Dead Jews do not work.'

'Food!' Hannah whispered to herself, and the dream she'd had came back to her: all that Seder food and the familiar faces around the table, faces she could almost – but not quite – name. She imagined the taste of the roast beef and saliva filled her mouth. Standing, she smoothed down the wrinkled skirt of her dress and looked around for Gitl.

Gitl was bending over one of the lowest shelves. Hannah recognized her by the awful red print dress. Hurrying over, Hannah called out, 'Food, Gitl! They'll give us food. If we hurry. At last!'

Gitl stood up slowly and stared past Hannah to the door as if she did not see her. Her mouth whispered. something but no sound came out, and her hands clenched and unclenched into fists.

Something forced Hannah to bend down and stare into the shelf. Little Tzipporah lay curled in a ball, her finger in her mouth like a stopper in a bottle. There was a fly on her cheek. Hannah reached out to brush it off.

'Do not touch her,' Gitl said.

'But . . .' Hannah's hand hovered over the child's cheek and the fly that would not leave.

'I said: *Do not touch her!*' Gitl's voice was strangely hoarse.

Hannah still reached toward the fly, unbelieving, and Gitl grabbed her hand, spinning her around. She slapped Hannah's face twice. 'Do not,' *slap*, 'touch her,' *slap*.

Then, as suddenly, she put her arms around Hannah with such force, Hannah gasped. Gitl buried her face against Hannah's shoulder, sobbing, 'Yitzchak . . . what will I say . . . Tzipporah . . . he must be told . . . what can I . . . *monsters!*'

It was all Hannah could do to free her arms enough so that she could pat Gitl's shorn head, touching it with as much tenderness as she could muster, while her cheeks still burned from the unwarranted slaps.

They were the last ones out of the barracks. Even Fayge had managed to get onto the proper food line before them, with the help of one of the women from her village. Emerging from the building, blinking into the noon sun, Hannah saw that Gitl's eyes were dry but they still held a reserve of some awful unspoken anger.

The line moved quickly, silently. At the first table, a girl handed them each a metal bowl. Plain-faced, with a broad forehead and deep-set brown eyes, she greeted them with a smile as if they were old friends. Hannah guessed she couldn't have been more than ten years old, yet her face seemed ageless.

'You must take good care of your bowl,' the girl said to them. It was obvious she had recited these same words to each group of newcomers, yet her voice held a sweetness and a patience quite out of keeping with the information she delivered. 'I call them Every Bowls because they are everything to us. Without the

105

bowl, you cannot have food, you cannot wash, you cannot drink. Memorize your bowl – its dents, its shape. Always know where you have put it. There are no replacements.' She winked at Hannah. 'That is the official speech. My mother, may she rest in peace, used to give it and now I take her place. If you meet me tonight after supper, I will tell you the rest. And if you cannot find me, ask anyone for Rivka. *Rivka.*'

Too exhausted to react, Hannah nodded and held up her bowl for its dipperful of watery potato soup. At the next table, she was given a small slab of dark bread. She began to eat even before she left the line. She was too hungry to eat slowly, and the soup and bread were gone before she had time to look around.

After the meal, the *zugangi* were lined up again in what seemed to Hannah to be a totally arbitrary order, orchestrated by the same three-fingered woman. She dealt out slaps and pushes with such fervor that they all did her bidding without protest. Hannah managed to dodge a slap. The slap meant for her hit Shifre, who cried out in pain and was hit again for the noise. Hannah bent her shoulders over against Shifre's muffled sobbing, guilty because she had been the cause of it, relieved because the blow had not fallen upon her.

When they were lined up to the woman's satisfaction, she nodded abruptly and walked to the front to address them.

'You wonder what to expect from now on?' she asked. 'I will tell you what to expect. Hard work, that is what. Hard work and more hard work. And punishment if you do not perform well and on time, without complaints.'

Her speech was short enough that Hannah took a deep breath in relief. She was just starting to relax when a man in a dark uniform jangling with medals walked over to the woman. The woman bowed her head and then looked up at the gathering of prisoners, smiling an awful warning.

Standing for a long moment, hands behind his back, the officer silently surveyed them. Hannah felt as if he were looking deep inside her, toting up her abilities, guessing at her chances. Someone else she knew stood that way. *Mr . . . Mr . . . Mr. Unsward.* She had the name and could almost see him in her mind's eye, but she couldn't remember who he was, only that he was someone who stood up in front of a group and shook his head just like that. She wondered if she should smile at the officer and whether it might help. Sometimes it worked in school. With Mr. Unsward. *In school!'* There – she had it, an elusive slip of memory. Then as quickly it faded, replaced by another, much more vivid memory: little Tzipporah, lying still on the low shelf, her finger corked so finally in her mouth. That image stopped any chance of a smile.

The officer cleared his throat. 'You will have discipline,' he said suddenly, without preamble. 'You will work hard. You will never answer back, complain, or question. You will not try to escape. You will do this for the Fatherland. You will do it – or you will die.' The officer turned smartly on his heel and left.

Then the three-fingered woman came forward to

tell them about the work that lay ahead and what they were to expect each day.

Above them, a quartet of swallows dipped and circled, twittering madly as they plunged after insects. There was a drone of machinery somewhere off to the right. In the distance, beyond another long row of barracks, Hannah could see a single strand of smoke rising against the bright spring sky, curling endlessly out of a tall chimney stack.

Once again it occurred to her that there was something she was not remembering, something terribly important to her, to all of them. She wondered if Gitl would know what it was, and resolved to ask her. But the raucous swallows, the woman's droning commands, the ground bass of the machinery mesmerized her. She could feel her eyelids starting to close. To stop herself from falling asleep on her feet, she threw her head back suddenly and took a deep breath.

Out of the corner of her eye she glimpsed Gitl. Then, without moving her head farther, only her eyes, she managed to find Fayge. She was standing halfway down the line, her face paper white and her eyes fully closed. She swayed where she stood. Behind her was Esther and beside Esther was Shifre, her lashless eyes even stranger-looking under the shaved head. Hannah remembered them, remembered each and every thing they had said to her in the forest. She remembered the forest. And remembered she had told them stories. But the stories – those she could not remember, and it bothered her that she could not.

She'd seen men running to get into a line behind

them during the first moments of the assembly, but she hadn't dared turn around then. Even now she was afraid to look. Would Shmuel be there? Yitzchak? Would Rabbi Boruch, the *badchan*, the members of the *klezmer* band? Would Mr. Unsward?

'Gitl,' she whispered out of the side of her mouth, low enough so that the woman in blue couldn't hear her. 'Gitl.'

Gitl touched her hand. 'Chaya,' she whispered back, so fiercely, it sounded like a promise. Or a command.

14

THAT EVENING, after another meal of watery soup and a small piece of bread, the girl Rivka found Hannah. She already had Esther and Shifre in tow. The other two girls looked as uneasy as Hannah felt, out in the open, with the watchtowers spaced every hundred feet along the barbed wire fences staring down at them.

'Do not be afraid,' Rivka said quickly. 'We have little to fear in the night. Any 'Choosing' is done during the day. They do not run the gas at night. They let us out for an hour each evening for enforced recreation. If you are alive now, this minute, it is enough.'

'What do you mean *it is enough?*' Esther said, her voice rising in pitch. 'My father is missing. My grandmother died on that train. I cannot find any of my aunts. Yente and Rachel are gone.'

Rivka shook her head sadly. 'I have been here a year, and in that time my mother and my sisters, my father and brother have gone there.' She pointed to the far smokestack. 'My mother because she was coughing too badly to work, my sisters – three younger than me – because they would not leave her side. My father and my brother Saul because they were too angry, too strong, too outspoken. Now my brother Wolfe is left, but he is a *Sonderkommando*, one of the walking dead. He might as well be with them. We all have such stories. It is a brutal arithmetic. But I – I am alive. You are alive. As long as we breathe, we can see and hear. As long as we can remember, all those gone before are alive inside us.'

Esther started to turn away, but Rivka caught her arm. 'Listen to me. Please. You must listen if you wish to stay alive. I know the things you need to know in this place. There is the *malach ha-mavis*, the Angel of Death, hovering overhead. But we can fool him if we follow the rules.'

'Who are you to tell us anything?' Shifre asked. 'What makes you an authority?'

'This is my authority,' Rivka said sternly, holding up her arm so that the number showed. J18202. '*J* because I am – like you – a Jew. The *1* is for me because I am alone. The *8* is for my family because there were eight of us when we lived in our village. And the *2* because that is all that are left now, me and Wolfe, who believes himself to be a *0*. But I love him no matter what he is forced to do. And when we are free and this is over, we will be *2* again. God will allow it.'

'God is not here,' Hannah said. 'The *badchan* was right. This is the Devil's place.'

'God made the Devil, so God is here, too,' Rivka said.

'*Pilpul*, a man's game,' Shifre said.

Rivka smiled. 'I play the man's game. I play the Devil's game. I play God's game. And so I stay alive.

111

Alive I can help you. Dead I am no help to you at all.'

Without meaning to, Hannah smiled back.

'Good,' Rivka said, nodding. 'If you smile, you will stay alive.'

'Then tell us, Rivka, about all these rules,' Hannah said.

'First, you may call me Rivka and I may call you by your names, but remember my number as you remember your own. You must learn to read the numbers as you would a name. There are good numbers and bad numbers.'

'What do you mean?' Shifre asked.

Esther walked away from them, shaking her head and humming loudly as if to drown out the sound of Rivka's voice.

'Esther . . . ,' Shifre called.

'Leave her,' said Rivka. 'Leave her. Sometimes people get like that. They stop listening. They stop seeing. It is as if they decide that life is not worth fighting for. We call them *musselmen*. It is sad. Very sad. I will be sorry if your friend chooses that, but if she does, I will let her. And you must let her as well.'

Shifre nodded. 'I understand.'

'I don't,' Hannah said. 'You can't just let her go.'

'You will have to,' Rivka said. 'It is one of the hard things you must do to stay alive. To let people go. To know when to fight and when not to. To know who to talk to and who to avoid. Listen. Never stand next to someone with a *G* in her number. She is a Greek and Greeks do not speak Yiddish and do not understand German. Greek Jews disappear quickly.'

'They become these *musselmen*?' Shifre asked.

'They become . . . gone,' Rivka answered. 'Because they do not understand commands fast enough, they do not react fast enough. Anyone standing next to them may be gone with them, sent off to Lilith's Cave alongside a Greek. And here is another rule . . .'

'Those aren't *rules*' Hannah argued. 'Those are crazinesses.'

'Nevertheless, you must learn them,' Rivka said. 'See my number? It is lower than yours. Someone with a number like mine has been here a long time. We are survivors. We can tell you things. Read the numbers. My lower number tells you I can *organize* things.'

'*Organize?*' Hannah shook her head. 'What do you mean?'

'*Organize*,' Rivka said. 'As I have *organized* some shoes for you, and not wooden clogs, either. And sweaters. You will need them because the nights are cold still. And if you need medicines, though we have few of them, even in the hospital – and you do not want to go there if you can help it – you must find Sarah the Lubliner, J11177. She works in the sorting shed and sometimes she can *organize* ointments from the pockets of coats or valises. And sometimes pills. I think some bandages, too, though you can wear them only where no one can see or Sarah would be in trouble. The commandant likes her. She was a singer in Lublin. In the cafés. He has her sing at suppertime when he visits.'

Hannah and Shifre stared at Rivka as she rattled on.

113

It was like a waterfall of information, Hannah thought. How could she take it all in and be safe?

'And you must never go near that,' Rivka said, turning suddenly and pointing way across the compound to a large wooden fence. There was a black handleless door. Beyond the fence loomed the smokestack. 'We call that the door to Lilith's Cave, the cave of death's bride. If you go through that door, you do not come out again.'

'Lilith . . . ,' Hannah muttered as if remembering a Story.

'But the most important thing for you to know is the midden,' Rivka said.

'The garbage dump?' Shifre and Hannah asked together.

'Yes. Commandant Breuer is not supposed to allow children under fourteen in the camp. So whenever he comes to inspect things, the children have to disappear. What he does not see does not exist. The best hiding place is in the midden. None of the Germans go there. It is beneath them. Oh, they know the children are hiding in it, of course, but they pretend it is too dirty, too disgusting. So they do not look. Even Breuer really knows.'

'We have to go *into* the midden?' Hannah was clearly shocked.

'Not us. We look old enough. I am only ten but everybody thinks I am older. And you two can surely pass. You have . . .' She motioned toward her own undeveloped chest. 'So we do not have to be *dumped*. But it is our duty to help the little ones.'

114

'The Germans are right.' Shifre said. 'It is disgust-ing.'

'Disgusting? Garbage can be Paradise,' Rivka said. 'One of my sisters could not run fast enough to disappear into the midden's sanctuary. They sent her with my mother, right through the door into Lilith's Cave. I can still hear her calling to me to save her, to hide her . . .'

Hannah suddenly heard a child's voice, as if from far away, saying, *'Hannah, look where I hid. . .'* She couldn't think who the child was. Or who Hannah was. Her head hurt with trying to remember.

'She went on the line and was gone,' Rivka finished.

Hannah stared at Rivka. 'What line?'

'The line. The one drawn by the *malach ha-mavis*, the Angel of Death. The one into . . .' Her face pale, her coffee-colored eyes unreadable, Rivka stopped.

Hannah nodded slowly, suddenly sure of one thing, as if she had known it all her life: 'Into the gas ovens,' she whispered.

'Oh, Chaya, not another one of your stories,' Shifre said, her eyes wide and full of fear.

Rivka led them to her own barracks, three buildings away from the place where the *zugangi* were housed. There were names carved on the bunks and magazine advertisements stuck onto nails in the walls, as if the women had tried to personalize the place, but it did not help. These barracks were as starkly unwelcoming as theirs.

From under her sleeping shelf, Rivka pulled out a

115

pile of shoes. Quickly, she sorted through them until she found three pairs, two of which matched exactly and a third that was at least the same size and style, though one shoe was dark maroon and the other brown. The shoes were badly scuffed and worn through at the toes, but wearable. 'I hope these fit, or at least are close enough.'

'Why don't they give us back our own shoes?' Hannah asked.

'Because the good shoes get sent to Germany,' Rivka said. 'But one does not ask *why* here.'

'Another rule?' Hannah asked.

'And a good one,' Rivka said. 'It is better not to know some things. Knowing the wrong things can make you crazy.'

'No stockings?' Shifre said.

'You are lucky to have real shoes,' Rivka answered. 'And not just clogs. When I got here, I had to run around for months on wooden clogs my mother carved for me.'

'Wooden shoes!' Hannah said.

Rivka smiled. 'Never mind. I shall keep trying for better shoes for all of us.' She looked down at her own shoes. The right was so badly worn at the heel, her foot showed through. 'At least now it is spring and we have time to look. Last month was bad. There was snow and frost. Masha from Krakow, J16689, lost two toes and there were many cases of frostbite. Bad cases, bad enough to go to the hospital. The Dark Angel goes there first. You are lucky.'

'*Lucky!*' Hannah muttered.

'Yes, lucky' Rivka said, sounding as if she were beginning to lose patience. 'We count our luck with a different measure here in the camp.'

Shifre stared silently at the shoes she held in her hand but Hannah shook her head slowly over and over.

'Now tell me your names.'

'Shifre.'

Rivka nodded.

'Chaya,' Hannah whispered, the name sounding strange in her mouth, foreign. Then she bit her lip and, remembering Rivka's explanation, held up her arm. 'And also *J* for Jew. And *1* for me, alone. I am very, very much alone. And *9* is for . . . well, in English it is pronounced 'nine,' which is like the German word for *no*. No, I will not die here. Not now. Not in my sleep like . . . little . . . little children.'

'How do you know English?' Shifre asked. 'Did you learn it in your school in Lublin?'

'You went to school?' Rivka asked, a kind of awe in her voice.

'No. Yes. I don't remember,' Hannah said, surprised at the whine in her voice.

Rivka put her hand out, touching Hannah gently on the arm, stroking the number with two fingers, ever so gently. 'It happens sometimes. We forget because remembering is so painful. But memory will return, when you are ready for it. Go on, Chaya – J19 . . .'

Hannah nodded. 'J – I – 9 – 7. *Seven* is for – for each and every day of the week I stay alive. One day at a time. Then *2* for Gitl and Shmuel, who are here in this

117

place, too.'

'Her aunt and uncle,' Shifre added. 'She is living with them . . . *was* living with them.'

'And *4* for . . . for . . .' She stopped, closed her eyes, and thought a minute. Four was such a comforting number, a familiar number, a family number. She wasn't sure why. 'And *4* is for my family, I think. I almost remember them. If I close my eyes they are there, hovering within sight. But when I open my eyes, they are gone.'

'It happens,' Rivka said.

'Her parents died of cholera. In Lublin. It was a great tragedy, Tante Gitl said,' Shifre volunteered. 'But maybe . . .' She looked around the barracks. 'Maybe it was a great blessing.'

'No,' Hannah said suddenly. 'No. Not them. Not in Lublin. Not those parents. At least not exactly.'

This time it was Shifre who put her hand on Hannah's arm, though she spoke to Rivka. 'Do not mind her ramblings. She was terribly sick before she came to live with Gitl and Shmuel. Once the doctors thought she had died, but they brought her back. She was in the hospital for weeks. She says odd things.'

'And *1*,' Hannah continued as if she had never been interrupted, 'because I am all alone. Here. In this place. In this . . . this time!' She ended triumphantly, though part of her wondered what she had meant.

'Chaya says she will live,' Rivka said to Shifre. 'Wherever else her mind may wander, she has said it. I hope she means it. And now, Shifre, tell me your number in the same way. It will help us both remember. After that, we will find your other friend.'

'Esther? But you said she was hopeless.'

'Esther! She is not a *musselman* yet. There is still hope for her. But if she does not get her shoes and sweater and a lesson in camp manners, she will not be long for even this world, I tell you.'

But they could not find Esther in the short hour before they were herded back into the barracks. Shifre took the mismatched shoes for her and Hannah the sweater, and then they entered the *zugangi* barracks with the others for the first long night in camp.

Hannah slipped uneasily into sleep, with the sounds of seventy women around her. Some of them were noisy sleepers, punctuating their dreams with snores. One or two cried out sharply in their sleep. And one woman wept throughout the night, low horrible sobs that rose in pitch until someone got up and comforted her. Then she would begin her sobbing again, slowly gathering volume and strength.

Hannah's dreams were filled with the sobs, but in the dreams they were cries of joy. She dreamed she was in a schoolyard where girls in blue dresses and blue pants with brightly colored sweaters hooked arms and laughed, shutting her out from their group. When she woke, she was crying. Her upper arms, which had served as her pillow, were wet. The sweater she had used for a blanket had slipped to the floor. She could not remember the dream.

15

IN THE MORNING, after roll call and breakfast were over, they got their first lesson at the midden.

'Commandant!' a man called across the wire fence from the men's camp.

'Commandant coming!' A woman took up the cry.

'He is coming,' Rivka said urgently to Hannah and Shifre, who were standing near the cauldrons, where they had been helping dish out the watery soup. 'Do what I do.'

Rivka put her hands up to her mouth as if shouting, but instead made a penetrating clucking noise by placing her tongue against the roof of her mouth. From all over the camp came the same clicking, as if crazed crickets had invaded the place. The small children, alerted by the sound, came scrambling from everywhere. They raced toward the midden heap behind the barracks. Even the camp guards joined in, alternately clucking and laughing, waving the children on toward the garbage pile. The largest children carried the littlest ones in their arms. There were about thirty in all.

Hannah watched, amazed at their speed. When they got to the midden, they skinned out of their clothes and dove naked into the dump.

Suddenly Hannah noticed that one of the camp babies was still cradled in a washtub. Without stopping to ask, she grabbed it up and ran with the child into the middle of the midden. Garbage slipped along her bare legs.

She waded through a mixture of old rags, used bandages, the emptied-out waste of the slop buckets. The midden smell was overwhelming. Though she'd already gotten used to the pervasive camp smell, a cloudy musk that seemed to hang over everything, a mix of sweat and fear and sickness and the ever-present smoke that stained the sky, the smell in the midden was worse. She closed her eyes, and lowered herself into the garbage, the baby clutched in her arms.

When the all-clear clucking finally came, Hannah emerged from the heap with the baby, who was cooing. She scrubbed them both off with a rag until the child's mother, Leye, came running over.

'I will murder that Elihu Krupnik. Where is he? He is supposed to take her in. And look! You left her clothes on. They are filthy.' Leye's face was contorted with anger.

'No thanks?' Rivka asked. 'Leye, she saved the baby.'

Leye stared for a moment at Hannah, as if seeing her for the first time. Then, as if making an effort, she smiled. 'I will *organize* some water,' she said, leaving the filthy baby in Hannah's filthy arms.

'That means "thank you,"' Rivka said.

Hannah stared after Leye. 'I think . . .,' she said

slowly, 'I think I prefer the water to the thanks.'

That night, she washed out her dress with the cup of water, hanging it like a curtain from her sleeping shelf. Now she understood why the children had all stripped off their clothes, dropping them like bright rags on the sandy ground. She'd worried that the clothing would be gaudy signals to the commandant, but clearly he already knew – as did the guards – where the children hid. It was all some kind of awful game. But she'd been too scared to stop and too shy to undress out in the open like that, especially while the memory of her naked hours waiting for the shower still brought a blush to her face. Especially as the guards, some in their late teens, had all been laughing nearby.

As she fell asleep, she was sure the smell of the midden had gotten into her pores; that there was not enough water in the camp – in all of Poland – to wash her clean.

The days quickly became routine: roll call, breakfast, work, lunch, work, supper, work. The meals were all watery potato soup and occasionally bread, hard and crusty. Then they had a precious hour before they were locked in their barracks for the night.

The work was the mindless sort. Some of it was meant to keep the camp itself running: cleaning the barracks, the guards' houses, the hospital, the kitchen. Cutting and hauling wood for the stoves. Building more barracks, more privies. But most of the workers were used in the sorting sheds, stacking the clothing and suitcases and possessions stolen from the prisoners, dividing them into piles to be sent back to Germany.

Still, Hannah was glad of the routine. As long as she knew what to expect, she wasn't frightened. What was more frightening was the unknown: the occasional corpse hanging on the gate without an explanation, the swift kick by the *blokova* for no reason.

She and Shifre were set to work with Rivka in the kitchen hauling water in large buckets from the pump, spooning out the meager meals, washing the giant cauldrons in which the soup cooked, scrubbing the walls and floors. It was hard work, harder than Hannah could ever remember doing. Her hands and knees held no memory of such work. It was endless. And repetitive. But it was not without its rewards. Occasionally they were able to scrape out an extra bit of food for themselves and the little ones while cleaning the pots, burned pieces of potatoes that had stuck to the bottom. Even burned pieces tasted wonderful, better even than beef. She thought she remembered beef.

'She gave the *blokova* a gold ring she *organized* to get you in here,' Leye explained, wiping her hands on a rag and nodding her head in Rivka's direction. Leye was the head of the kitchen crew; her arms were always splotchy and stained. But it was a good job, for she could keep her baby with her. 'Otherwise that one . . .' and she spit on the ground to show her disapproval of the three-fingered woman, '. . . she would have had you hauling wood with the men. And you

123

would never have lasted because you are a city girl. It is in your hands. Not a country girl like Shifre. We outlast you every time.'

When Hannah tried to thank Rivka, the girl only smiled and shrugged away the thanks. 'My mother, may she rest in peace, always said *a nemer iz nisht keyn geber*, a taker is not a giver. And a giver is not a taker either. Keep your thanks. And hand it on.' She said it gently, as if embarrassed.

Hannah understood her embarrassment and didn't mention it again, but she *did* try to pass it on. She began saving the softer insides of the bread, slipping it to Reuven when she could. Yitzchak's little boy was so thin and sad-looking, still wondering where his sister had gone, that she could not resist him. She even tried giving him her whole bread, meal after meal, until Gitl found out.

'You cannot help the child by starving yourself,' Gitl said. 'Besides, with those big blue eyes, he will have many to help him. And that smile . . .'

Hannah bit her lip. Those big blue eyes and the luminous, infrequent smiles reminded her of someone she couldn't name.

'But you – you are still a growing girl, Chaya. You must take care of you.' She folded Hannah's hands around the bread and pushed her away from Reuven. 'Go, finish your kitchen duties. I will take Reuven with me.'

Hannah turned away reluctantly, as if she had somehow failed Rivka. As she did so, she saw that Gitl had given the child her own bread and half her soup besides.

It was on the third day in the camp that Commandant Breuer came again, this time – word was whispered around the camp – for a Choosing.

His black car drove right up the middle of the camp, between the rows of barracks, the flag on the aerial snapping merrily. The driver got out, opened the rear door, and stood at attention.

'What *is* a Choosing?' Hannah asked Rivka out of the side of her mouth as they waited beside the cauldrons they were cleaning. She didn't know why, but she could feel sweat running down her dress, even though it was a cool day, as if her body knew something it wasn't telling her mind.

There was no movement from the midden pile, where the bright shorts and blouses of the children marked their passage. The commandant strode past without giving the dump a glance.

Rivka hissed Hannah quiet and ran a finger across her own throat, the same signal that the peasants had made in the fields when the cattle cars passed them by. Hannah knew that signal. She just didn't know what it meant . . . exactly. She shivered.

The commandant was a small, handsome man, so clean-shaven his face seemed burnished. His cheekbones had a sharp edge and there was a cleft in his chin. He stopped for a moment in front of Hannah, Rivka, and Shifre. Hannah felt sweat run down her sides.

The commandant smiled, pinched Rivka's cheek,

then went on. Behind him was a man with a clipboard and a piece of paper. They walked without stopping again, straight to the far end of the compound. The door banged behind them ominously.

Rivka let out a ragged breath, and turned to Hannah. 'Anyone who cannot get out of bed today will be chosen,' she said. Her voice was soft but matter-of-fact.

'Chosen for what?' Hannah asked, though she'd already guessed.

'Chosen for processing.'

'You mean chosen for death,' Hannah said. Then suddenly she added, 'Hansel, let out your finger, that I may see if you are fat or lean.'

'Do not use that word aloud,' Rivka cautioned.

'Which word?' asked Hannah. 'Finger? Fat? Lean?'

Rivka sighed. 'Death,' she said.

'But why?' asked Shifre, her pale face taking color from the question. 'Why will some be chosen?'

'Because they cannot work,' said Rivka. 'And work . . .' Her voice became very quiet and, for the first time, Hannah heard a bitterness in it. 'Because work *macht frei*.'

'And because he enjoys it!' added Leye, coming over to see why they were not working.

'But do not let them hear you use the word *death*. Do not let them hear you use the word *corpse*. Not even if one lies at your feet,' Rivka warned. 'A person is not killed here, but chosen. They are not cremated in the ovens, they are *processed*. There are no corpses, only pieces of *drek*, only *shmattes*, rags.'

126

'But why?' asked Hannah.

'Why?' Leye said. 'Because what is not recorded cannot be blamed. Because that is what *they* want. So that is how it must be. Quickly, back to work.'

No sooner had they begun scrubbing again than the door to the hospital opened and Commandant Breuer emerged, still smiling, but broader this time. As he and his aide passed by, Hannah could see the paper on the clipboard was now covered with numbers and names.

The commandant reminded her of someone. A picture perhaps. A moving picture. She'd seen a smiling face like that somewhere.

'Dr. . . Dr. Mengele,' she said suddenly. 'The Angel of Auschwitz.' As suddenly as she knew it, the reference was gone.

'No,' Rivka said, puzzled, 'his name is Breuer. Why did you say that?'

'I told you she says strange things,' Shifre put in.

Hannah looked down at her hands. They were trembling. 'I don't know why I said it. Am I becoming a *musselman*? Am I going mad?'

No one answered.

Gitl had been working in the sorting shed, where mountains of clothes and shoes, mounds of books and toys and household goods from the suitcases and bags were divided up. It was also the place where men and women could talk together, so there was a quick, quiet trading of information from the women's camp to the men's and back again.

That night, Gitl shared the news with the others of the *zugangi* barracks. 'All the clothes and shoes in good condition go straight to Germany. And we get what is left. But look what I took for you, Chayaleh.' She held up a blue scarf.

'*Organized*. You *organized* it, Tante Gitl,' Shifre cried out, her hands up with delight.

The women all laughed, the first time such a sound had rippled through the barracks since they had arrived. 'Yes, she *organized* it.'

Gitl looked up, pursed her lips for a moment, then smiled. 'All right. I *organized* it.'

'How did you do it, Gitl!' someone called.

'You can bet she did not ask!' came an answer.

Gitl nodded, stretching the scarf between her hands. '*Az m'fraygt a shyle iz trayf.* '

Hannah translated mentally, 'If you ask permission, the answer is no.' She remembered suddenly another phrase, from somewhere else, almost like it: 'It's easier to ask for forgiveness than permission.' She had a brief memory of it printed on something. Like a shirt.

'So,' said Esther's mother, a self-satisfied look on her face, 'we may be *zugangi*, but we already know how to *organize*.'

Esther looked longingly at the blue scarf, and hummed quietly to herself.

Gitl handed the scarf to Hannah. 'To replace the blue ribbons,' she said softly.

'The blue ribbons?' For a moment, Hannah couldn't remember them. Then she did.

'And because today is your birthday,' Gitl added.

'Her birthday!' cried Shifre. 'You did not tell me.'

Hannah shook her head. 'My birthday is . . . is in the winter. In . . . in *February*.' The word sat strangely on her mouth.

'What nonsense is this?' asked Gitl, her hands on her hips. 'And what kind of word is *February*? They taught you to count the days by the Christian calendar in Lublin?' She turned to look at the women who were circled around them. 'You think I do not know my own niece's birthday? And did I send a present every year?'

'Of course you know,' a gray-haired woman called out.

'I remember the day she was born,' said another. 'You told me in the synagogue, all happy with the idea. You were only thirteen, you said, and already an aunt.'

'So,' Gitl said, turning to face Hannah.

Her certainty overrode Hannah's own. Besides, she asked herself, who knew what day it was, what year, in this place?

'Thank you, Gitl,' she whispered. 'It's the best present I've ever had, I think. The only one I remember, anyway.'

'Oh, my dear child,' Gitl said, pulling her close, 'thank God that your father and mother are not alive to see you now.'

Caught in Gitl's embrace, Hannah suddenly remembered the little house in the shtetl and the big, embracing arms of Shmuel. 'What of Shmuel?' she said. 'And Yitzchak? Are they . . . well?'

129

Gitl sat on a low shelf bed and pulled Hannah down next to her. The circle of women closed in, eager for news.

Gitl nodded. 'Now listen. Shmuel is working with the crew that cuts wood, but it is all right. It is what he knows how to do and he is strong. With him are Yitzchak the butcher and Gedaliah and Natan Borodnik and their cousin Nemuel. Tzadik the cobbler is doing what he has always done, making shoes and belts. They have a cobbler's shop there. He is making a fine pair of riding boots for the commandant. Size five.'

'That is a woman's size!' Esther's mother said with a laugh.

'Yes, and they have made up a little rhyme about it. Listen, I will tell it to you:

Breuer wears a lady's shoe,
What a cock-a-doodle-do.'

The women began to giggle; Hannah didn't understand the humor.

Gitl held up her hand and the laughter stopped. 'And from Viosk, Naftali the goldsmith is making rings on order for all the SS men. He is a very sick man but they like his work so much, they are leaving him alone.'

'And where does he get the gold?' asked a woman in a stained green dress.

'From the valises, idiot,' someone else answered.

'From our fingers,' Fayge said suddenly, the first time she had spoken in days. She held up her hands so

130

that everyone could see that they were bare. 'From our ears.'

'From our dead,' Gitl whispered. Hannah wondered whether anyone else heard her.

'What about the others?' Esther's mother asked.

'I do not remember anything more,' Gitl said softly.

'What about the rabbi?' asked a woman with a hare-lip. 'What about Rabbi Boruch?'

Gitl did not answer.

Fayge knelt down in front of her, putting her hands on Gitl's skirt. 'We are sisters, Gitl,' she said. 'I am your brother's wife. You must tell me about my father.'

Gitl closed her eyes and pursed her lips. For a long moment she did not speak, but her mouth opened and shut as if there were words trying to come out. At last she said, 'Chosen. Yesterday. *Boruch dayan emes.*'

Fayge opened her mouth to scream. The woman in the green dress clapped her hand over Fayge's mouth, stifling the scream, pulling her onto the sandy floor. Three other women wrapped their arms around her as well, rocking back and forth with her silent sobs.

'Chosen,' Gitl said explosively, her eyes still closed. 'Along with Zadek the tailor, the *badchan*, the butcher from Viosk, and two dozen others. And the *rendar*.'

'*Why!*' asked Hannah.

'The rabbi was in the hospital. His heart was broken. Zadek, too. He had been beaten almost to death. The *badchan* because he chose to go. They say he said, 'This is not a place for a fool, where there are idiots in charge.' And the others whose names I do not

remember for crimes I do not know. And the *rendar*
. . .'

'With all his money he could not buy his way out?'
asked Esther's mother.

'In this place he is just a Jew, like the rest of us,'
said Gitl. 'Like the least of us.'

'He's a *shmatte* now,' said Hannah, remembering
Rivka's word.

Gitl opened her eyes and slapped Hannah's face
without warning. 'That may be camp talk out there,
but in here, we say the prayer for the dead properly,
like good Jews.'

'Gitl the Bear,' someone murmured.

Hannah looked up, hand on her smarting cheek.
She could not find the speaker, so spoke to them all.
'Gitl is right,' she said, her cheek burning. 'Gitl is
right.'

Gitl began reciting the *Kaddish*, rocking back and
forth on the sleeping shelf with the sonorous words,
and the prayer was like the tolling of a death bell. The
rest joined her at once. Hannah found she was saying
the words along with them, even though her mind
didn't seem to have any memory of the prayer: *Yis-ga-
dal v'yis-ka-dash sh'may ra-bo* . . .

16

THE FIRST CHOOSING had been the hardest, Hannah thought later. After that, it merely became part of the routine. And if you didn't stand too near the Greeks or work too slowly or say the wrong word or speak too loudly or annoy a guard or threaten the *blokova* or stumble badly or fall ill, the chances were that this time you wouldn't be Chosen. This time.

Part of her revolted against the insanity of the rules. Part of her was grateful. In a world of chaos, any guidelines helped. And she knew that each day she remained alive, *she remained alive*. One plus one plus one. The Devil's arithmetic, Gitl called it.

And so one day eroded into the next. Her memories became camp memories only: the day a guard gave her a piece of sausage and asked for nothing in return. The morning a new shipment of *zugangi* arrived. The morning a new shipment *didn't* arrive. The afternoon Gitl *organized* a rope and the children all played jumping games after dinner. And that same night when redheaded Masha from Krakow hanged herself with the jump rope, having learned that her husband and seventeen-year-old son had gone up the smokestack.

It was on a sunny afternoon, as Hannah cleaned out cauldrons with Shifre, that Hannah asked dreamily, 'What is your favorite food? If you could have anything in the world.'

They were in the tipped-over pots on their hands and knees, scraping off bits of burned potato that still clung stubbornly to the vast pot bottom.

Shifre backed out of the cauldron, wiping one dirty hand across her cheek. She thought a moment before answering. It was not a new question. They had been asking each other variations of the same thing for weeks.

'An orange, I think,' she said slowly. That was a change. Usually she said an egg.

'An orange,' Hannah echoed, pleased with the novelty. 'I'd forgotten oranges.'

'Or an egg.'

'Boiled?'

'Or fried.' They were back to their regular conversation.

'Or scrambled?'

'Or an omelet.'

'How about . . . pizza!' Hannah said suddenly.

'What is *pizza*?' Shifre asked.

'It's . . . it's . . . I don't know,' Hannah said miserably, fingers in her mouth, blurring the words. 'I can't remember. I can only remember potato soup.'

'You can remember eggs,' Shifre said.

'No, I can't. Not pizza, not eggs either. Only potato soup and hard brown bread. That's all I can remember.' She popped a piece of the burned potato scraping into her mouth.

'Well, do not cry over this *pizza*. Tell me about it.'

'I can't,' Hannah said. 'And I'm not crying over the thing, whatever it is. I'm crying because I can't remember *what* it is. I can't remember anything.'

'You can remember the shtetl,' Shifre said. 'And Lublin.'

'That's the trouble,' said Hannah. 'I can't.'

Just then Rivka came out of the kitchen and shook her finger at Hannah. 'No tears,' she said. 'If the *blokova* sees you crying . . .'

'That three-fingered bi . . .' Hannah stopped herself in time. It was a dangerous habit to fall into, calling the *blokova* names. One might be Chosen for doing such a thing.

'If she loses control of her *zugangi*, she will be a two-fingered whatever-you-call-her,' said Rivka, smiling.

'What do you mean?' Hannah and Shifre asked together.

'How do you think she lost those other fingers?'

Hannah mused. 'I thought maybe she'd been born that way.'

Holding up her own hand and wriggling the fingers, Rivka pointed to one. 'She lost control and a whole group of *zugangi* rioted. That was right before I got here. They were sent through Lilith's Cave and she lost one finger. Then she lost control and six *zugangi* hanged themselves one night, my aunt Sarah among them. Aunt Sarah had been sick for a long time and could no longer disguise it. She knew she was to be

135

sent to the hospital. Everyone really sick in the hospital goes up the stack. So she said to my mother, "*I* will do the choosing, not them. God will understand."' Rivka smiled. 'A second finger. I wish Aunt Sarah could have seen the *blokova*'s face in the morning. When they took the finger.'

'Maybe *we* could do something to help the *blokova* balance her hand. Three is such an unlucky number,' Shifre said.

Rivka shook her head. 'Too dangerous,' she said. 'Let the grown-ups make their plans.'

'What plans?' asked Hannah.

'Oh,' Rivka said mysteriously, 'there are always grown-up plans.'

'What plans?' Hannah and Shifre asked together. But before Rivka could answer, a shout from the gate end of the compound riveted them.

'Commandant!'

'But he was just through yesterday,' Hannah said in a nervous whisper. 'He's not due for at least another few days.'

Ignoring her, Rivka already had her hands to her mouth, making the clucking sound to warn the children. Shifre, too, was signaling.

'It's not *fair!*' Hannah complained, her voice rising into a whine.

Shifre nudged her angrily, and Hannah began to cluck as the little ones scrambled for the midden pile.

The first two in were a brother and a sister, seven and eight years old. They left green and blue shorts and shirts at the edge of the dump. Next came a nine-year-old girl carrying a baby. She shucked off her shoes as she ran and, holding the baby under one arm, tore off its shirt. When she set the naked baby down by the side of the pile in order to get out of her own dress, the child immediately began crawling toward the midden on its own.

Like spawning fish, the children came from everywhere to dive into the pile. They waded or crept in one after another while the horrible clucking continued and overhead the swallows, alerted to a feast of insects, dipped and soared.

Hannah finally heard the commandant's car, then saw it as it barreled toward them, down the long bare avenue between the barracks. It moved relentlessly toward the hospital, which squatted at the compound's end.

The car had just passed the *zugangi* barracks when the hospital door opened and a small thin boy limped down the steps, his right knee bloody and his blue eyes ringed with dirt. He was wiping his hands on his shirt. When he looked up and saw the car bearing down on him, despite the desperate clucking from all around, he froze, staring.

'Reuven!' Hannah cried out. 'Run! Run to the midden!' But the boy didn't move and she felt a sudden coldness strike through her as if an ice dagger had been plunged into her belly.

'*Gottenyu!*' Rivka whispered.

Shifre, who had been looking at the midden with its bright flags of clothing, heard Hannah's shout and turned. She grabbed Hannah's hand, squeezing it until there was no feeling left.

The car slowed, then stopped. Commandant Breuer himself got out of the car. He walked toward Reuven and the child could not look at him, staring instead at Hannah, his hand outstretched toward her. Big tears ran down his cheeks, but he cried without a sound.

'He knows,' Hannah whispered.

'Hush!' Rivka said.

The commandant looked down at the boy. 'Have you hurt yourself, my child?' he asked, his voice deadly soft.

Hannah moved forward a half-step and Rivka jerked her back.

'Let me see,' Breuer said. He took a white handkerchief out of his pocket and touched it to Reuven's bloody knee thoughtfully. 'And where is your mother?'

When Reuven didn't answer, Hannah stepped forward. 'Please, sir, his mother is dead.'

Rivka gasped. Hannah heard her and added hastily, 'She died years ago, when he was born.'

The commandant stood up and stared at her, his eyes gray and unreadable. 'Are you his sister?'

She shook her head dumbly, afraid to say more.

'That is good. For you.' Breuer bent down and wrapped the handkerchief around the boy's knee, knotting it gently with firm, practiced hands. Then he picked Reuven up. 'A boy your age should be with his mother,' he said, smiling. 'So I shall be sure you go to her.' He handed Reuven to his driver, who was waiting by the car door. Then, without another word,

Breuer went up the stairs to the hospital and closed the door so quietly they could not tell when it was finally shut.

That evening, the sky was red and black with the fire and smoke. The latest arrivals in the cattle cars had not been placed in barracks. The camp was full. The newcomers had been shipped directly to processing, a change in routine that frightened even the long-termers.

Rumors swept the camp. 'A shipment from Holland,' some said. 'A shipment from Silesia.' No one knew for sure.

But Reuven did not come back. Not that evening. Not that night.

'Not ever,' Hannah muttered to herself as she watched the smoke curling up, writing its long numbers against the stone-colored sky. 'And it's my fault.'

'Why is it your fault?' Rivka asked.

'I should have said he was my brother.'

'Then you would not be here either. It would not have helped Reuven.'

'He is dead.' Hannah said the word aloud curiously, as if understanding it for the first time. 'Dead.'

'Do not say that word.'

'Monsters!' Hannah said suddenly. 'Gitl is right. We are all monsters.'

'*We* are the victims,' Rivka said. '*They* are the monsters.'

'We are all monsters,' Hannah said, 'because we are letting it happen.' She said it not as if she believed it

139

but as if she were repeating something she had heard.

'God is letting it happen,' Rivka said. 'But there is a reason. We cannot see it yet. Like the binding of Isaac. My father always said that the universe is a great circle and we – we only see a small piece of the arc. God is no monster, whatever you think now. There is a reason.'

Hannah scuffed the ground with her foot. 'We should fight,' she said. 'We should go down fighting.'

Rivka smiled sadly. 'What would we fight with?'

'With guns.'

'We have no guns.'

'With knives.'

'Where are our knives?'

'With – with something.'

Rivka put her arm around Hannah's shoulder. 'Come. There is more work to be done.'

'Work is not fighting.'

'You want to be a hero, like Joshua at Jericho, like Samson against the Philistines.' She smiled again.

'I want to be a hero like . . .' Hannah thought a minute but she could think of no one.

'Who?'

'I don't know.'

'My mother said, before she . . . died . . . that it is much harder to live this way and to die this way than to go out shooting. Much harder. Chaya, you are a hero. I am a hero.' Rivka stared for a moment at the sky and the curling smoke. 'We are all heroes here.'

That night Fayge began to speak, as if the words so

long dammed up had risen to flood. She told a story she had heard from her father, about the great Ba'al Shem Tov. It was set in the time when he was a boy named Israel and *his* father warned him: 'Know, my son, that the enemy will always be with you. He will be in the shadow of your dreams and in your living flesh, for he is the other part of yourself. There will be times when he will surround you with walls of darkness. But remember always that your soul is secure to you, for your soul is entire, and that he cannot enter your soul, for your soul is part of God.' Fayge's voice rose and fell as she told how young Israel led a small band of children against a werewolf whose heart was Satan's. And in the end, when Israel walked straight into the werewolf's body and held its awful dark heart in his hand, 'shivering and jerking like a fish out of water,' Fayge said, her own hand moving in the same way, that awful heart was filled with 'immeasurable pain. A pain that began before time and would endure forever.'

She whispered the story as the night enfolded them. 'Then Israel took pity on the heart and gave it freedom. He placed it upon the earth and the earth opened and swallowed the black heart into itself.'

A sigh ran around the barrack and Hannah's was the deepest of all. *A werewolf*, she thought. *That's where we are now. In the belly of the werewolf. But where, where is its dark pain-filled heart?* She was still sighing when she slipped into sleep.

17

'THERE IS A PLAN,' Gitl whispered. 'and Yitzchak and Shmuel are part of it.' She had crept onto the sleeping shelf, putting her arms around Hannah and speaking very softly into her ear. 'You must not be afraid, but you must not tell anyone. I am a part of it, too.'

Hannah didn't move.

Gitl's voice tickled her ear. 'The reason I am telling you this is that you are our only flesh and blood. Our only link with the past. If something happens to us, you must remember. Promise me, Chaya, you will remember.'

Hannah's lips moved but no sound came out.

'Promise.'

'I will remember.' The words forced themselves out through her stiffened lips.

'Good.'

'What plan?' Hannah managed to ask.

'If I tell you, you might say.'

'Never.'

'You would not mean to, but it could slip out.'

'Not even if *afile . . .*'

'*Afile brenen un brutn* . . . even if you should be burned and roasted. Here that is not a proverb to be spoken aloud.'

Horrified at what she'd said, Hannah felt herself begin to giggle. It was a hysterical reaction, but she couldn't seem to control herself.

'Nevertheless,' Gitl ended, 'I will not tell you.'

'When?' Hannah whispered.

'You will know.'

The horn signaled morning roll call and Gitl rolled off the shelf. Hannah followed, stood, and stared at her.

'Is it . . . is it because of Reuven?' she asked quietly.

'For Yitzchak it is. Who else does he have left, poor man? He adored those children,' Gitl said.

'But why you? Why Shmuel?'

'If not us, who? If not now, when?' Gitl smiled.

'I think I've heard those words before,' Hannah said slowly.

'You will hear them again,' Gitl promised. 'Now we must not talk about this anymore.'

And yet for all of Gitl's promises, nothing seemed to happen. The days' routines were as before, the only change being the constant redness of the sky as train-loads of nameless *zugangi* were shipped along the rails of death. Still the camp seemed curiously lightened because of it, as if everyone knew that as long as others were processed, *they* would not be. A simple bit of mathematics, like subtraction, where one taken away from the top line becomes one added on to the bottom. The Devil's arithmetic.

'When?' she whispered at night to Gitl.

'You will know,' Gitl always answered. 'You will know.'

And yet, when it finally happened, Hannah was surprised that she hadn't known, hadn't even suspected. There had been no signs or portents, no secret signals. Just an ordinary day in the camp and at night she went to bed on the hard, coverless shelf trying to remember sheets and pillows and quilts while all around her in the black barrack she heard the breathy sounds of sleeping women.

A hand on her back and over her mouth startled her so, she was too surprised to protest.

'Chaya, it is now,' Gitl's voice whispered in her ear. 'Nod if you understand.'

She nodded, opening her eyes wide though it was too dark to see anything. 'The plan,' she said, her words hot on Gitl's palm. She sat up abruptly and just missed smacking her head on the upper shelf.

Gitl took her hand away. 'Follow me,' she whispered.

'Am I part of the plan?'

'Of course, child. Did you think we would leave you in this hell?'

They crept to the door and Hannah could feel her heart thudding madly. It was warm in the barrack, yet she felt cold.

'Here,' Gitl whispered, shoving something into her hands.

Hannah looked down. She could see nothing in the dark, but she realized she was holding a pair of shoes.

'We'll put them on outside.'

They paused at the door, then Gitl eased it open slowly. It protested mildly.

'It's not locked!' Hannah said, shocked.

'Some guards can be bribed,' Gitl whispered. 'Give me your hand.'

Slipping her hand into Gitl's, Hannah held back for a moment. 'What about Fayge? Shmuel wouldn't go without Fayge.'

Gitl's hand on hers tightened. 'Fayge says she prefers the dark wolf she knows to the dark one she does not.'

'Even with Shmuel going? But she loves him.'

'She has come to love her next bowl of soup more,' Gitl said. 'Now hush.'

They slipped through the door, shut it, and locked it from the outside with a too-loud *snick*. Hannah shivered at the sound and took Gitl's hand again, ice on ice.

'We meet behind the midden,' Gitl whispered. 'No more talking now.'

Hannah looked up. There was no moon. Above them, in the cloudless sky, stars were scattered as thick as sand. A small, warm breeze blew across the compound. Night insects chirruped. Hannah took a deep breath. The air was sweet-smelling, fresh, new. A dog barked suddenly and a harsh voice quieted it with a command.

Gitl pulled Hannah back against the barrack's wall.

Hannah could feel the fear threatening to scream out of her, so she dropped the shoes and put both hands over her mouth, effectively gagging herself. There was a wetness under her arms, between her legs, down her back. She moaned.

And then there came a shout. A shot. And another. And another, rumbling, staccato. A man began to scream, high-pitched and horrible. He called a single phrase over and over and over. *'Ribono shel-oylam.'*

'Quickly!' Gitl whispered hoarsely. 'It is ruined. Before the lights. Come.'

As she spoke, great spotlights raked the compound, missing them by inches and seeking the outer perimeter of wire fence and mine fields and the woods beyond, where Hannah thought she saw shadows chasing shadows into the dark trees.

Gitl dragged her back to the barrack's door, slid the bolt open with one hand, and shoved Hannah inside with the other. They both sank gratefully to the floor.

'What is it?' the *blokova*'s voice called out from her private room.

Hannah's mouth opened. What could they say? They would be found out. They would be Chosen.

'I went to get my bowl to relieve myself,' Gitl called, her voice incredibly calm. 'And then shots began outside and I was so frightened, I fell to the floor, dropping the bowl.' She pushed Hannah away from her as she spoke.

Crawling on her hands and knees, Hannah made it back across the room to her sleeping shelf. She lifted herself onto it gratefully, trembling so hard she was sure she would wake everyone.

'You Jews,' the *blokova*'s voice drawled sleepily, 'you can never do anything quietly, or efficiently.' That is why the Germans will finish you all off. If you have to relieve yourself, wait until the morning or do it in your bed. Or you shall have to deal with me.'

'Yes, *blokova*,' Gitl answered.

'And get to bed,' the *blokova* added unnecessirily.

Instead of going to her own shelf, Gitl crowded in with Hannah, hugging her so tightly that Hannah could hardly breathe. Yet she was glad not to have to lie there alone. Leaning back against Gitl, Hannah could feel the woman shaking with silent sobs.

Then a sudden, awful thought came to her. She couldn't turn over with Gitl there on the shelf, so she whispered to the wall: 'Gitl, Gitl, please.'

At last Gitl heard. 'What is it?'

'The shoes, Gitl, I dropped the shoes outside. They'll know it was me out there. What will I do? What will I do?'

'Do?' the breathy voice whispered into her ear. 'Do? Why, you will do nothing, my darling child. Those were not your shoes. They were the *blokova*'s. I took them from outside her door because you deserved a better pair for such a difficult journey. They will discover *her* shoes in the morning.' She began to laugh, muffling it against Hannah's back, a sound so close to sobbing that Hannah could not tell the difference.

18

THE ROLL CALL in the morning was held under a brilliant sun and a sky so blue it hurt the eyes. The woods on the other side of the barbed wire fence burst with birdsong. Commandant Breuer himself stood at the front of the assembly, flanked by SS guards. Before him were six men in chains.

Hannah recognized only Shmuel and the violin player from the *klezmer* band. The other four men were strangers to her. They had all been badly beaten and two could not stand.

'Yitzchak . . . ,' she whispered.

Beside her Gitl was silent.

'Yitzchak . . . ,' she tried again.

'Hush.'

The commandant stared around the compound as if his mind were on other matters. Once he even looked up at the sky. At last he turned his attention to Shmuel, who stood chin thrust out defiantly.

Shmuel spat.

A guard hit him with the butt end of his gun in the stomach and Shmuel went down on his knees, but he made no sound.

148

'These men . . . ,' Breuer began, 'these pieces of, in your Jew language, *drek* tried to escape last night. Escape! And where would they go? To the mine fields? To the woods to starve? To the town where no right-thinking Pole would give them shelter? This camp is in the middle of nowhere, remember that. *You* are in the middle of nowhere. All that gives you life is work – and my good wishes. Do you understand?' He glanced around as if daring any of them to challenge him.

They were silent.

'I see I have been too easy on you. I have made you into my pets. That is what they call you, you know: Breuer's dirty little pets. The other transports, they do not come here and sleep in barracks and have three meals every single day. They are not cared for in a modern hospital. They are not given clothes and shoes.' He held up a pair of woman's shoes and Hannah tried not to stare at them, but they drew her eyes. 'No, they are processed at once, as has been ordered from Berlin. They are part of the Final Solution to the Jewish Problem. But you, my little pets, I have let you live to work. And see how you reward your master.'

He walked over to the violinist, who had been pushed to his knees by a guard. Pushing the man's head back, Breuer spoke directly to him, but in a voice that carried around the compound: 'I let *you* play music because it is said that music feeds the gods. Well, now you shall feed your god.' He signaled to his men. 'Move them to the wall.'

There was a protesting sound from the crowd, a strange undercurrent of moaning. Hannah realized

149

suddenly that she was one of the moaners, though she didn't know what going to the wall meant. Something awful, that she knew.

'Silence!' Breuer said, his voice hardly raised at all. 'If you are silent, I will let you watch.'

They were all silent. Not, Hannah thought, because they wanted to watch, but because they wanted to be witnesses. And because they had no other choice.

The guards dragged the men to a solid wall that stood next to the gate. The wall was pocked with holes and dark stains. To the right and above, the sign ARBEIT MACHT FREI swung creakingly in the wind. Birds cried out merrily from the woods and the tops of the trees danced to rhythms all their own.

The six men were lined up with their backs to the wall, four standing and two sitting. Shmuel alone smiled.

Slowly the soldiers raised their guns and Hannah bit her lip to keep from crying aloud.

'*Shema Yisrael, Adonai Eloheynu . . . ,*' the violinist began in a clear voice. The other men at the wall joined him.

But Shmuel was silent, searching through the watching crowd, that same strange smile on his face. At last his lips moved and Hannah read the word there.

'Fayge.'

'Shmuel!' came a loud wail, and Fayge pushed through the crowd, flinging herself at his feet. She lifted her face to his and smiled. 'The sky is our canopy. God's canopy. The sky.'

He bent down and kissed the top of her head as the guns roared, a loud volley that drowned out birdsong and wind and screams.

When it was silent at last, the commandant threw the shoes on top of Fayge's body. 'Let them all go up the stack,' he said. 'Call the *Kommandos. Schnell!*'

The soldiers marched off to the side of the compound, except for one, who opened the door into Lilith's Cave. Out came ten men in green coveralls. Though she'd heard of them, feared them, mourned them, Hannah had never actually seen any of them before. One, hardly more than a boy, put his fingers to his lips and a shrill whistle pierced the air. The *Kommandos* lifted their heads at the sound and in mocking parody of the soldiers marched over to the wall. They began to drag the dead bodies back toward the gate.

The boy who had whistled stooped down and picked up Fayge in his arms. His beardless face was grim, but there was no sign of sorrow or horror there. Still he carried Fayge as one might carry a loved one, with conscious tenderness and pride.

Rivka whispered to no one in particular, 'That one, carrying Fayge, that is my brother, Wolfe.'

The *blokova* came forward, a wooden spoon in her hand with which she dealt out blows right and left. '*Schnell. Schnell.* Scum. There is work to do, much work.' Her voice held a note of hysteria. The hand with the spoon didn't rest, but her other hand was held stiffly by her side. It was wrapped in a broad bandage, the white stained with fresh blood.

151

'Gitl . . . ,' Hannah said as they walked back toward the kitchen. 'Did you see?'

'I saw,' Gitl said, her voice ragged. 'I saw everything.

'I mean, did you see that Yitzchak wasn't there?'

Gitl turned, took Hannah by the arms, and stared at her. 'Yitzchak?'

'He wasn't there. He wasn't in the lineup either.'

'Hush,' Gitl said, turning away, but her voice held a measure of hope. 'Hush.'

Hannah said no more, but in her mind's eye she saw a swift shadow racing into the dark trees. She smiled with the memory.

Later that afternoon, the cauldrons all set for cooking, Hannah walked with Rivka and Shifre to the water pump. Esther was there already, filling a bucket in slow motion for the women in the sewing shop. She had lost a lot of weight, the dress hung in loose folds on her frail body, her eyes were dead.

Overhead the swallows dipped down to catch bugs rising from the ground. Then they soared back up beyond the barracks. Hannah watched them for a moment, scarcely breathing. It was as if all nature ignored what went on in the camp. There were brilliant sunsets and soft breezes. Around the commandant's house, bright flowers were teased by the wind. Once she'd seen a fox cross the meadow to disappear into the forest. If this had been in a book, she thought, the skies would be weeping, the swallows mourning by the smokestack.

Her mouth twisted at the irony of it and she turned to the three girls at the water pump. Suddenly, with great clarity, she saw another scene superimposed upon it: two laughing girls at a water fountain dressed in bright blue pants and cotton sweaters. They were splashing water on each other. A bell rang to call them to class. Hannah blinked, but the image held.

Drawing a deep breath, she forced herself to bring the camp back into focus; it was like turning a camera lens. One way she could see the water fountain, the other way the pump. Her heart was thudding under the thin gray dress. She was afraid to move. And then suddenly she made up her mind.

'Listen,' she said to the girls at the pump, 'I have a story to tell you.'

'A story?' Shifre looked up, her light-lashed eyes bright. 'You have not told us a story since the first day. At the . . .' She hesitated a minute, afraid to name the memory, afraid a guard might hear and, somehow, steal it away.

'*At the wedding*,' Hannah said. 'Funny how saying it brings it back. *At the wedding. At school. At home.*'

'Tell the story,' Rivka pleaded. 'I would like to hear it.' For the first time she sounded like the ten-year-old she was.

Hannah nodded. 'This isn't a once-upon-a-time story,' she said. 'This is about now – and the future.'

'I do not want a story about now,' Esther said slowly. 'There is too much now.'

'And not enough future,' Shifre added.

153

Hannah moved close to them. 'Now – six million Jews will die in camps like this. *Die!* There, I've said the word. Does it make it more real? Or less? And how do I know six million will die? I'm not sure how, but I do.'

'Six million?' Shifre said. 'That's impossible. There are not six million Jews in the whole world.'

'Six million,' Hannah said, 'but that's not all the Jews there are. In the end, in the future, there will be Jews still. And there will be Israel, a Jewish state, where there will be a Jewish president and a Jewish senate. And in America, Jewish movie stars.'

'I do not believe you,' Esther said. 'Not six million.'

'You must believe me,' Hannah said, 'because I remember.'

'How can you remember what has not happened yet?' asked Rivka. 'Memory does not work that way – forward. It only works backward. Yours is not a memory. It is a dream.'

'It's not a dream, though,' Hannah said. 'It's as if I have three memories, one on top of another. I remember living with Gitl and Shmuel.'

'May he rest in peace,' Rivka said.

'May they all rest in peace,' Hannah added.

'And Lublin,' put in Shifre. 'You remember Lublin.'

'Yes, there is Lublin, but that memory is like a story I've been told. I don't remember Lublin, but I remember being there. And then there's my memory of the future. It's very strong and real now, as if the more I try to remember, the more I do. Memory on memory on memory, like a layer cake.'

'I remember cake,' Shifre said.

'Impossible,' Esther said.

'Even crazy,' Rivka pointed out.

'Nevertheless,' Hannah said, 'I remember. And you – you must remember, too, so that whoever of us survives this place will carry the message into that future.'

'What message?' Rivka asked, her voice breathy and low.

'That we *will* survive. The Jews. That what happens here must never happen again,' Hannah said. 'That . . .'

'That four girls are talking and not working,' interrupted a harsh voice.

They looked up. Standing over them was a new guard, his nose reddened from the sun. He had a strange, pleased look on his face. 'I have been told that the ones who do not work are to go over there.' He pointed to the gate.

'No!' Rivka cried. 'We were working. We were.' She held up the empty bucket.

The guard dismissed her pleas with a wave of his hand, and all four of them held their breath, waiting.

'I was told that we need three more Jews to make up a full load. Commandant Breuer believes in efficiency and our units do not work well with short loads. So I was sent to find three of the commandant's pets who were *not* working. He told me – personally – to make up the load.'

'We *were* working,' Shifre begged, her words tumbling out in a rush. 'And we are healthy. We are

155

healthy hard workers. You never take healthy hard workers. It is one of the rules. Never.'

The guard smiled again. 'Since Commandant Breuer makes the rules, I guess he can change the rules. But why are you worrying so, *Liebchen?* I only need three. Perhaps I won't take you.' He looked over the girls slowly, the smile still on his face. 'I'll take you. You are the least *healthy.*' He pointed to Esther, who almost fell forward in front of him, as if someone had suddenly kicked her in the back of the knees.

Shifre drew in a great, loud breath and closed her eyes.

'And you,' he said, playfully putting his finger on Shifre's nose, almost as if he were flirting with her, 'because you protest too much after all. And . . . and . . .'

Hannah let out her breath as slowly as she dared. She did nothing to call attention to herself. To stay alive one more day, one more hour, one more minute, that was all any of them thought of. It was all they could hope for. Rivka was right. What she had was not a memory but a dream.

'. . . and you, with the babushka, like a little old lady. I'll take you, too.' He pointed to Rivka, winked at Hannah, then turned and marched smartly toward the gate, confident that the chosen girls would follow.

Rivka gave Hannah a quick hug. 'Who will remember for you now?' she whispered.

Hannah said nothing. The memories of Lublin and the shtetl and the camp itself suddenly seemed like the dreams. She lived, had lived, would live in the future – she, or someone with whom she shared memories. But Rivka had only now.

Without thinking through the why of it, Hannah snatched the kerchief off Rivka's head. 'Run!' she whispered. 'Run to the midden, run to the barracks, run to the kitchen. The guard is new. He won't know the difference. One Jew is the same as another to him. Run for your life, Rivka. Run for your future. Run. Run. Run. And remember.'

As she spoke, she shoved Rivka away, untied the knot of the kerchief with trembling fingers, and retied it about her own head. Then, as Rivka's footsteps faded behind her, she walked purposefully, head high, after Shifre and Esther.

When she caught up with them, she put her arms around their waists as if they were three schoolgirls just walking in the yard.

'Let me tell you a story,' she said quietly, ignoring the fact that they were both weeping, Shifre loudly and Esther with short little gasps. 'A story I know you both will love.'

The strength in her voice quieted them and they began to listen even as they walked.

'It is about a girl. An ordinary sort of girl named Hannah Stern who lives in New Rochelle. Not Old Rochelle. There is no Old Rochelle, you see. Just New Rochelle. It is in an America where pictures come across a cable, moving pictures right into your living room and . . .' She stopped as the dark door into Lilith's Cave opened before them. 'And where one day, I bet, a Jewish girl will be president if she wants to be.

Are you ready, now? Ready or not, here we come . . .'

Then all three of them took deep, ragged breaths and walked in through the door into endless night.

19

WHEN THE DARK finally resolved itself, Hannah found she was looking across an empty hall at a green door marked 4N.

'*Four for the four members of my family*,' Hannah thought. '*And N for New Rochelle.* 'She couldn't see Shifre or Esther anywhere. They had slipped away without a farewell. She almost called out their names, thought better of it, and turned to look behind her.

There was a large table set with a white cloth. The table was piled high with food: matzah, roast beef, hardboiled eggs, goblets of deep red wine. Seven adults and a little blond boy were sitting there, their mouths opened expectantly.

'Well, Hannah?' said the old man at the head of the table. 'Is he coming?'

Hannah turned back and looked down the long, dark hall. It was still empty. 'There's no one there,' she whispered. 'No one.'

'Then come back to the table and shut the door,' called out the other old man. 'There's a draft. You know your Aunt Rose gets these chills.'

'Sam, don't hurry the child so. She's doing her part.'

The woman who spoke had a plain face lit up by a special smile. 'Come, sweetheart, sit by Aunt Eva.' She patted an empty chair next to her, then reached over and picked up her glass of wine. 'You look so white, Hannahleh. Like death. How can we fix that?' She raised her glass, looked at Hannah. '*L'chaim*. To life.' She took a sip.

Hannah slipped into the chair, knowing it was the one the family reserved for the prophet Elijah, who slipped through the centuries like a fish through water. She watched all the grown-ups raise their glasses.

'*L'chaim.*'

Aunt Eva turned toward her, smiling. Her sweater was pushed back beyond her wrist. As she raised the glass again, Hannah noticed the number on her arm: J18202.

'Hannahleh, you're staring,' whispered Aunt Eva as the talk began around the table: Uncle Sam arguing about the price of new cars, Grandpa Will complaining about the latest government scandal, her mother asking Aunt Rose about a book.

'Staring?' She repeated the word without understanding.

'Yes, at my arm. At the number. Does it frighten you still? You've never let me explain it to you and your mother hates me to talk of it. Still, if you want me to . . .'

Hannah touched the number on her aunt's arm with surprising gentleness, whispering, 'No, no, please, let me explain it to you.' For a moment she was silent. Then she said: '*J* is for Jew. And *1* because you were alone, alone of the *8* who had been in your family, though *2* was the actual number of them alive. Your brother was a *Kommando*, one of the Jews forced to tend the ovens, to handle the dead, so he thought he was a *0*.' She looked up at Eva, who was staring at her. 'Oh! Your brother. Grandpa Will. That must have been him carrying Fayge. So that's why . . .'

Aunt Eva closed her eyes for a moment, as if thinking or remembering. Then she whispered back, 'His name was Wolfe. Wolfe! And the irony of it was that he was as gentle as a lamb. He changed his name when we came to America. We all changed our names. To forget. Remembering was too painful. But to forget was impossible.' Her coffee brown eyes opened again. 'Go on, child.'

Hannah took her hand from her aunt's arm and dropped it into the safety of her own lap. She couldn't look at her aunt any more, that familiar, unfamiliar, plain, beautiful face. 'You said . . . ,' she whispered, '. . . you said that when things were over, you would be two again forever. J18202.'

They sat for a long moment in silence while the talk and laughter at the table dipped and soared about them like swallows.

At last Hannah looked up. Her aunt was staring at her, as if really seeing her for the first time. 'Aunt Eva . . .' Hannah began and Eva's hand touched her on the lips firmly, as if to stop her mouth from saying what had to be said.

'In my village, in the camp . . . in the past,' Eva said,

161

'I was called Rivka.'

Hannah nodded and took her aunt's fingers from her lips. She said, in a voice much louder than she had intended, so loud that the entire table hushed at its sound, 'I remember. Oh, I remember.'

Epilogue

AUNT EVA TOLD HANNAH the end of the story much later, when the two of them were alone, because no one else would ever have believed them. She said that, of all the villagers young Chaya had come to the camp with that spring, only two were alive at the end of the war. Yitzchak, who had indeed escaped, had lived in the forest with the partisans, fighting the Germans. And Gitl. When the camp had been liberated in 1945, Gitl weighed only seventy-three pounds because she had insisted on sharing her rations with the children. But she was alive.

The *blokova* and all the villagers from Viosk were dead, but among the living, besides Gitl, Yitzchak, and Rivka, were Leye and her baby, a solemn three-year-old.

Gitl and Yitzchak had emigrated to Israel, where they lived, close friends, until well into their seventies. Neither of them ever married. Yitzchak became a politician, a member of the Israeli senate, the Knesset. Gitl, known throughout the country as Tante Gitl and Gitl the Bear, organized a rescue mission dedicated to salvaging the lives of young survivors and locating the remnants of their families. It later became an adoption agency, the finest in the Mideast. She called it after her young niece, who had died a hero in the camps: CHAYA.

Life.

What is true about this book

ALTHOUGH THE STERNS' Seder is not strictly a traditional one, it is a mirror of the Seders my family used to hold. My Uncle Louis was the one who always said, 'And how do I know? Because I was there!' while hiding the *afikoman* in plain sight under his chair for the youngest to find and hide again. The word *Seder* literally means 'order,' but my family's religious life was not an orderly one. Like many American Jews, it was one of rough-and-tumble choices and lots of love. We were Jews because we were born Jewish, not because of following strict rules. When I had to memorize Hebrew and history for my Confirmation, I continually complained how tired I was of remembering. However, there is an orderly progress to a Seder that a perusal of its guidebook, the Haggadah, will show to the curious reader.

All the facts about the horrible routinization of evil in the camps is true: the nightmare journeys in cattle cars, the shaving of heads, the tattooing of numbers, the separation of families, the malnutrition, the *musselmen* and the *Kommandos*, the lack of proper clothing, the choosing of the victims for incineration. Even the midden pile comes from the camp experiences of one of my friends.

Only the characters are made up – Chaya, Gitl, Shmuel, Rivka, and the rest – though they are made up of the bits and pieces of true stories that got brought out by the pitiful handful of survivors.

The unnamed camp I have written about did not exist. Rather, it is an amalgam of the camps that did: Auschwitz, with its ironic sign ARBEIT MACHT FREI, was the worst of them, where in two and a half years two million Jews and two million Soviet prisoners-of-war, Polish political prisoners, Gypsies, and European non-Jews were gassed. Treblinka, where 840,000 Jews were killed. Chelmno, with its total of 360,000 Jews. Sobibor, with its 250,000. There were other camps, and their count is the Devil's arithmetic indeed: Belzec, Majdanek, Dachau, Birkenau, Bergen-Belsen, Buchenwald, Mauthausen, Ravensbruck. The toll is endless and anonymous. Whole families, whole villages, whole countrysides disappeared.

At the time of the Holocaust, it seemed impossible to imagine, for the scale of slaughter was difficult to grasp. Today, a lifetime later, we can echo Winston Churchill, who wrote: 'There is no doubt that this is probably the greatest and most horrible single crime ever committed in the whole history of the world.' And yet it is *still* impossible, unimaginable, difficult to grasp. Even with the facts in front of us, the numbers, the indelible photographs, the autobiographies, the wrists still bearing the long numbers, there are

166

people in the world who deny such things actually happened.

After all, how can we believe that human beings like ourselves – mothers, fathers, sisters, brothers – could visit upon their fellow humans such programmed misery, such a routine of torture, all couched in the language of manufacture: 'So many units delivered . . . operating at full capacity.' These were not *camps*, even though they were called so. These were *factories* designed for the effective murder of human beings.

There is no way that fiction can come close to touching how truly inhuman, alien, even satanic, was the efficient machinery of death at the camps. Nor how heroism had to be counted: not in resistance, which was worse than useless because it meant involving the deaths of even more innocents. 'Not to act,' Emmanuel Ringelblum, a Jewish historian of the Holocaust, has written, 'not to lift a hand against the Germans had become the quiet passive heroism of the common Jew.' That heroism – to resist being dehumanized, to simply outlive one's tormentors, to practice the quiet, everyday caring for one's equally tormented neighbors. To witness. To remember. These were the only victories of the camps.

Fiction cannot recite the numbing numbers, but it can be that witness, that memory. A storyteller can attempt to tell the human tale, can make a galaxy out of the chaos, can point to the fact that some people survived even as most people died. And can remind us that the swallows still sing around the smokestacks.

About the author

JANE YOLEN is one of America's most popular and prolific authors, writing everything from picture books to adult fiction. Jane was born in New York but now lives with her professor husband in a large white wooden house outside Northampton, Mass, where she had three children, now all grown up and obliging with a growing band of grandchildren. Every year Jane and her husband spend several months in St Andrew's, Scotland. Jane has won every major prize in Children's Books in the U.S. and has been described as 'The American Hans Andersen'.

Barn Owl Books – Recent Titles

The Spiral Stair – *Joan Aiken*
Giraffe thieves are about! Arabel and her raven have to act fast

Your Guess is as Good as Mine – *Bernard Ashley*
Nicky gets into a stranger's car by mistake

Voyage – *Adèle Geras*
Story of four young Russians sailing to the U.S. in 1904

Private – Keep Out! – *Gwen Grant*
Diary of the youngest of six in the 1940s

The Mustang Machine – *Chris Powling*
A magic bike sorts out the bullies

You're Thinking about Doughnuts – *Michael Rosen*
Frank is left alone in a scary museum at night

Jimmy Jelly – *Jacqueline Wilson*
A T.V. personality is confronted by his greatest fan

Leila's Magical Monster Party – *Ann Jungman*
Leila invites all the baddies to her party and they come!

The Gathering – *Isobelle Carmody*
Four young people and a ghost battle with a strange evil force

The Silver Crown – *Robert O'Brien*
A rare birthday present leads to an extraordinary guest

Playing Beatie Bow – *Ruth Park*
Exciting Australian time travel story in which Abigail learns about love